Sherlock Holmes and the Case of the London Dock Deaths

By

Margaret Walsh

Paperback ISBN 978-1-78705-636-7
ePub ISBN 978-1-78705-637-4
PDF ISBN 978-1-78705-638-1

Published by MX Publishing
335 Princess Park Manor, Royal Drive,
London, N11 3GX
www.mxpublishing.co.uk

Cover design by Brian Belanger

To Penny & David

Chapter One

The summer of 1889 was a particularly busy one for Holmes and myself, coming as it did off the back of the dreadful case of the Molly-Boy Murders.

London was seething like a stew pot in the heat. The Great London Dock Strike was in full swing. The poor men who worked the docks for a mere pittance had been organized into a union that was proving to be more than competent at holding the management of the various docks to account.

It was in this atmosphere of mingled heat and animosity that Michael Geraghty came to our door early one evening in late August.

Mrs. Hudson showed him into our rooms, and Holmes gestured for him to take a seat.

I took Michael Geraghty to be in his mid-thirties. He stood a little under 6 feet tall, with brown curly hair, gentle hazel eyes, and a warm and friendly smile that lightened his otherwise saturnine features.

Our client introduced himself and then said "I don't know who to turn to, Mr. Holmes. My brother is dead and I cannot get the police to take his death seriously."

"Tell me what happened," Holmes said, composing himself to listen.

"Three nights ago my brother, John Geraghty, was found dead in an alley near the Ten Bells pub in Whitechapel."

"Cause of death?" I asked.

"He was stabbed in the back, Doctor," Michael Geraghty replied. "The police in their wisdom have decided that my brother was just another drunken Irishman killed in a pub brawl. There was a perfunctory post mortem held, and no attempt made to find the killer or killers."

"You believe the case is not as the police describe it?" Holmes asked, brows raised in query.

"Yes, Mr. Holmes. For one thing, my brother had no reason to be anywhere near the Ten Bells. We live on Whitechapel High Street. There are pubs much closer to our house if he wished to drink. Which he did not. My brother, Mr. Holmes, was a blue-ribbon teetotaller. He never went near a pub. Indeed, he was quite vehemently against them. That evening he should have been at the wharf."

"The wharf?" Holmes asked.

"Duncran Wharf," Michael Geraghty replied. "It's only a small wharf. My grandfather started it when he brought the family here from Galway at the beginning of the famine. He'd operated something similar near Letterfrack. Grandfather was able to sell up, get the family out, and start again. But he could not afford much in London, the city being what it is. He purchased a run-down wharf with a few decrepit buildings, and even fewer customers."

Geraghty paused, a look of pride coming over his face. "Over the years he built up a reasonable little business. We don't make a fortune, but we do well enough. At least we did, until the strike started. I may end up having to sell to the London Docks people after all if the strike goes on much longer." He shook his head sadly.

I looked at Holmes, never a patient man at the best of times. I expected him to be annoyed at this rambling, but instead his face wore an expression of intense concentration.

"Let me get this straight, Mr. Geraghty," Holmes said. "Your brother was, essentially, found stabbed to death in a place he had no business being and the police have taken the expedient route in declaring his death as being the result of a pub brawl? Am I correct?"

"Yes, Mr. Holmes."

"Very well." Holmes's tone was brisk. "Leave me your card. We shall make some enquiries and I shall call upon you when I have something substantive to share."

Michael Geraghty got to his feet, his face breaking into a warm smile of relief. "Thank you, Mr. Holmes, and you too, Doctor Watson. My mother will be most relieved that you are taking our case."

As he shook both our hands, Holmes said, "Be aware that I may not be able to find out what happened."

"I am aware, sir. I am also aware that if you find nothing then it is because there is nothing to be found."

Michael Geraghty took his leave and we waited in silence until we heard to sound of the street door below closing.

Holmes walked to the window and stood watching our client walk away.

"Well, Watson, what do you make of it?"

"Mr. Geraghty may well be right about his brother having no business being near the Ten Bells; however, it would not be the first time a blue-ribboner has broken his pledge," I said.

"Very true, my friend." Holmes turned back from the window. "The Ten Bells is in H Division, and I have no contacts there."

"Time to call Lestrade?" I asked.

Holmes's tone was desert dry. "Utilise the police grapevine?"

"Why not?" I countered. "After all, it is not much different from your Baker Street Irregulars."

"Except the members are older, well-fed and, on the whole, smell better," Holmes retorted.

He was silent for a moment. "You are correct, my dear Watson, it is indeed time to call Lestrade. I shall send him a telegram and invite him to supper. He will be only too pleased to sample Mrs. Hudson's cooking again.

"You mean he does not come for the pleasure of our company?" Amusement coloured my tone.

"No doubt that is part of it, but the excellent food is the main attraction."

I smiled at Holmes. "I will go and send the telegram now, if you would like me to, and advise Mrs. Hudson of the possibility of an extra guest."

Holmes waved his thanks as he sank into his chair and reached for his pipe and the Persian slipper that held his tobacco.

Chapter Two

Lestrade arrived promptly at 7 o'clock. I heard him chatting with Mrs. Hudson as she let him into the building. Her laugh followed him up the stairs to our rooms.

The inspector was all smiles and bonhomie as he came in, thanking us warmly for the invitation.

Holmes waved his thanks away. "No need for thanks, Lestrade."

Lestrade grinned, causing his moustache to twitch. "You want something, don't you, Holmes?"

"Of course I do, but I have better manners than to bring it up before we have eaten, regardless of what my good Watson thinks," Holmes replied with some asperity.

Lestrade laughed and took the seat at the table that I directed him to. I seated myself, and Holmes joined us, just as Mrs. Hudson came in.

The next quarter hour or so was filled with the sounds of a hearty meal being enjoyed and desultory conversation only. Most of which related to the food.

Mrs. Hudson had furnished us with a fine repast of sausages with potatoes, peas, and onion gravy, along with her excellent homemade bread and sweet cream butter.

Finally replete, Lestrade sat back in his chair and beamed at us. "Now, tell me, what is it that you require my help with that you felt the need to bribe me with Mrs. Hudson's excellent cuisine?"

One of the reasons Holmes liked Lestrade, although he would never admit it, was the fact that Lestrade could be as blunt and uncompromising as himself. There was never a need to tread lightly with Lestrade as there was with some of the other London Metropolitan Police detectives.

Holmes got up from the table and crossed to his comfortable chair, gesturing for us to join him.

I paused long enough to pour us each a brandy, before I took my seat.

Lestrade settled into the remaining chair, brandy in hand, and looked at Holmes expectantly.

"Are you aware of a recent murder in Whitechapel, Lestrade?" Holmes asked.

Lestrade snorted. "There are always murders in Whitechapel, Holmes. You will have to be a little more specific than that."

"This one took place close to the Ten Bells. The victim was a young man. London Irish."

Lestrade frowned. "I vaguely recall hearing something about that. An open and shut case according to what I heard coming out of H Division, not to mention the coroner's court."

"The victim's brother does not think so."

Lestrade raised his eyebrows. "Oh?"

"He came to me today. The gentleman disagrees quite strongly with the decisions made by the police. And I admit that I tend to agree with him, based on the few things he told us."

Lestrade frowned. "You don't go jumping at shadows, Holmes. If you say something was wrong with the case, then I will believe you. What do you want from me?"

"Can you get me a copy of the official police report on the murder?"

Lestrade put his brandy down on the side table and withdrew his notebook from his pocket. "What was the victim's name?"

"The victim was John Geraghty. According to his brother, John did not drink, so had no reason to be anywhere near the Ten Bells. More to the point, he was supposed to be at the family's place of business at the time that he was killed."

Lestrade looked up from his writing. "Family's place of business?"

"They own and operate a small wharf on the Thames, hard by the larger London and St Katherine's Docks. The wharf is known as Duncran Wharf. It has been a family venture for three generations."

Lestrade looked back at his notebook with a frown. "That does not sound at all like what I was hearing. Nor does it sound like something Edmund would allow to slip by him."

"Edmund?" I asked.

"Inspector Edmund Reid," Lestrade replied. "Head of Detectives at H Division. A good man and a sound detective."

"I have heard of him," Holmes said. "He has a reputation for dogged police work. The man has a number of bravery awards, does he not?"

"He does," Lestrade confirmed. He closed his notebook and tucked it away in his pocket. "I shall see what I can do for you tomorrow. If I go burrowing around whilst I am off duty, someone will ask why."

"It is never a good idea to show your hand early," Holmes agreed.

Lestrade settled back in his seat and picked up his brandy. "Have you heard from Sir Lucas at all?"

Sir Lucas Catterick had been involved in our last case together and at its conclusion had moved, with his mother, grandmother, and cousin, to France. The only person to remain behind in London from the little group had been the elderly grandmother's companion, Dorothy Watts. After saving my life at the conclusion of the case, Dorothy had gone to work for Mycroft Holmes.

Holmes shook his head. When he spoke his tone held mild reproof. "You know that I rarely keep in contact with anyone from our past cases."

Lestrade grinned around his glass. "You keep in contact with me," he pointed out.

Holmes waved his glass at Lestrade. "You, Lestrade, have become as invaluable as my magnifying glass, my scrapbooks, and my doctor."

Lestrade laughed out loud and looked at me, his eyes twinkling with merriment. "How does it feel, Doctor Watson, to be included in such august company as Holmes's magnifying glass?"

I took a sip of my brandy in an attempt to hide the wry smile on my lips. "How does it feel, Lestrade? After all this time, if feels strangely normal. And what that says about me, I have no idea."

We chatted for a while about cases currently ongoing at Scotland Yard, none of which needed Holmes' particular talents. The talk got around to the difficulties of policing the docks areas with the strike going on.

"I only pray that we don't get a killer of the likes of the Whitechapel ripper, or that bastard Nathaniel Croft any time soon," Lestrade said gloomily. "We are stretched so thin that we have not got the manpower to run a big case. Not with the violence seething around the docks and into Wapping and Whitechapel."

"Surely, London could not be so unlucky as too have three such killers in the space of one year?" I said. "Cheer up, Lestrade. All will be well."

Lestrade smiled, a little sourly I thought, and took his leave.

Chapter Three

It was late the following morning before Lestrade returned to Baker Street.

He smiled distractedly at Mrs. Hudson as she poured him tea, and then waited until she had left to pull his notebook from his pocket.

"I was unable to bring the report, but I wrote down what were, to me, the most important features."

Holmes looked slightly cross. "What you deem to be important, Lestrade, and what is actually of importance are two vastly different things."

"I have done the best that I can, Holmes," Lestrade replied. He made as if to get to his feet, "But if you don't want my help…"

"Oh do sit down, Lestrade," I said. "And tell us what you found."

Lestrade sank back into his chair and consulted his notebook. "The report was quite concerning. It was immediately apparent to me that the officer who completed the report is anti-Irish. Not that uncommon, but disturbing in a police officer."

"How did you know he was anti-Irish?" I asked.

"He referred to the victim as a 'mick'," Lestrade replied in tones of deep distaste.

I frowned. "I am aware of that derogatory term for an Irishman, but I have no idea where it comes from."

"It comes from one man," Holmes replied. "An Irishman, of course, named Michael Barrett. He was hanged at Newgate in 1868 after being found guilty of causing an explosion in Clerkenwell that blew a hole in the wall of Clerkenwell Prison and killed several people."

Lestrade nodded. "The Clerkenwell Outrage the papers called it. Barrett was believed to be a member of the Irish Republican Brotherhood."

"After Barrett's execution," Holmes continued, "...his name began to be used as a derogatory term for an Irishman. Eventually Michael Barrett was shortened to Michael and then simply to Mick. The distasteful term that has Lestrade's dander up."

"I should have known it had something to do with crime, for you to know it," I said with some small amusement. "Thank you for the lesson."

Holmes waved the comment away and concentrated on Lestrade. "Apart from the abhorrent attitude of one policeman, what else is there?"

"Very little. It appears that it was dealt with by a uniformed sergeant. The detective branch was not even informed until the next day."

"Is that usual?" I asked.

"It depends upon the situation," Lestrade replied. "If the case is cut and dried, such as someone caught in the act, then yes. In the case of a man found dead in the street, then the detective department should have been alerted."

Lestrade frowned down at his notebook. "I wangled a look at the post-mortem report. Death was caused by knife wounds in the back. Two thrusts either side of the spine, one of which severed the renal artery. There were no signs that John Geraghty had been involved in a brawl. No bruising to the hands or face. Nor was he kicked as he lay upon the ground, which is common in a brawl."

"A severed renal artery would have meant that he bled out reasonably quickly," I commented.

"He was stabbed in the back," Holmes said. "No attempt was made to defend himself. John Geraghty knew his killer."

"How do you know that?" Lestrade asked.

"It is obvious, Lestrade. What sensible man would turn his back on a stranger in a dark alley?"

"Would a sensible man go down a dark alley with anyone in the first place?" I asked.

"If someone you know came up to you in the street and said they needed to talk to you, would you follow them wherever they led you?" Holmes asked.

I smiled wryly, knowing full well that if it were Holmes, or even Lestrade, I would do exactly that.

Holmes turned to Lestrade, "Was Geraghty found facing into or out of the alley?"

Lestrade consulted his notebook. "Facing towards the street."

"Obviously, the person either said what they had to say, or Geraghty did not like what he was hearing, and turned his back to leave."

"Whereupon the unknown killer stabbed him twice in said back," Lestrade breathed. "Holmes, you really are a marvel."

Holmes waved a hand. "Simply observation and deduction, Lestrade."

"Would the killer have got much blood on him?" Lestrade asked, looking at me.

I shook my head. "The severed renal artery would have bled into the abdominal cavity. There would have most probably been blood on the killer's hands and shirt cuffs, but no massive arterial spurt as you would get with the severing of the carotid or femoral arteries."

Lestrade sighed. "That being the case, the killer probably got away sight unseen. The area around the Ten Bells is badly lit. And no-one would have responded to the scream."

"He may not have screamed, Lestrade," I replied. "The blows would have felt like two sharp punches, followed by the sort of pain that leaves you breathless. Unconsciousness would have come shortly after that, followed soon after by death."

"Wonderful," Lestrade said morosely. "So our killer stabs a man in the back, steps over his victim and saunters away. Lovely."

"Our killer?" Holmes queried.

"Our killer," Lestrade replied firmly. "The London Metropolitan Police has done the wrong thing by John Geraghty and his family. That needs to be fixed, and the only way to do that is to find the killer and see him hang."

Holmes smiled slightly. "I do like the way you think, Lestrade. Your assistance on the case will be most welcome."

"What do we do now?" I asked.

"Our next move should be to have a chat with the policeman responsible for this obvious debacle," Holmes replied. "And perhaps a meeting with Inspector Reid. I should like to hear what he thinks of if all."

"I thought that might be the case, Holmes," Lestrade said. "To that end I have arranged for us to meet with Edmund this afternoon. Not at the station in Leman Street, but in the Ten Bells. I did not want the sergeant responsible getting the wind up if he knew both Scotland Yard and Sherlock Holmes were interested."

Holmes turned a look of approval upon Lestrade. "Well done, Inspector. Very well done indeed."

Chapter Four

The Ten Bells was busy when we arrived. Situated on bustling Commercial Street; close by Spitalfields Market, the main supplier of fresh fruit and vegetables for the East End of London, the pub was popular with market workers and locals alike.

We found Inspector Reid waiting in a parlour on the first floor; well away from the no doubt curious eyes at the bar. A grave faced man, with immaculately groomed beard and moustache, he rose from his seat at the small table and came forward to greet us.

"Giles! Good to see you again! You've been well?"

Lestrade clasped Reid's hand warmly. "Tolerably, Edmund." He turned towards us. "Edmund, may I introduce Mr. Sherlock Holmes and Doctor John Watson?"

Inspector Reid reached out and shook Holmes's hand and then mine. "A pleasure, gentlemen. I take a keen pleasure in your work, Mr. Holmes. You have a great gift."

"Thank you, Inspector Reid," Holmes replied, somewhat nonplussed. He was not used to such an enthusiastic reception from a police officer. I had to admit, that neither was I.

We took our seats at the table. Inspector Reid sent off for drinks and waited until we were comfortably arranged, drinks in front of us, before speaking.

"I was intrigued when Giles sent to me asking for this meeting. What can I do for the great Sherlock Holmes?"

"The Geraghty murder."

Reid's face clouded. "I should have supposed as much. I was not on duty at the time and not informed about it until the next day. It should not have been handled by uniformed men. They do not have the skills necessary."

He looked at my friend. "What brought that killing to your attention?"

"The deceased's brother," Holmes replied. "He is not happy with the police or the coroner's response, so he came to me for help."

"I cannot say that I blame him," Reid admitted. "How can I help?"

"Why was the murder not handed over to your detectives?" asked Holmes.

"It is a matter of time and men, Mr. Holmes. Edicts came down from above that all murders that are basically cut and dried, and do not need detective involvement, are to be handled by the uniformed branch."

"I have been given the details of both the police report and the post-mortem report. This murder was neither cut, nor particularly dried," said Holmes. "The investigating sergeant, for instance, appears to have a problem with Irishmen."

Reid winced. "Sergeant Albert Woods. Near to retirement age, and a curmudgeon with outdated views."

"Outdated views?" I asked.

"He still firmly believes the nonsense about the Irish being the missing link between apes and men," Reid replied.

It was my turn to wince. Charles Darwin's book "The Origin of the Species" had done much to fuel the English sense of superiority. John Beddoe's book "Races of Britain" printed three years later had just added to the blaze by claiming that the Irish and the Welsh were prognathous and closely related to Cromagnon man; the inference being that neither the Irish nor the Welsh were properly human.

Any decent doctor will tell you that is humbug. We all have the same organs in the same places, as the severing of John Geraghty's renal artery had so recently proved.

"So it would serve no purpose to question him?" Holmes asked.

"I believe not," Reid replied. "Woods is a surly beggar. He is barely civil to other policemen, let alone outsiders. I'm afraid you will need to find other avenues of enquiry, Mr. Holmes."

Holmes shrugged. He did not seem particularly put out by Inspector Reid's observation. "No matter. It is unlikely that he could tell us anything useful anyway."

Reid rose from his seat. "I really must be getting back to the station. A pleasure to see you again, Giles, and to meet you gentlemen. Any help you need with your investigation, Mr. Holmes, just send a note to me at Leman Street. I will see that you get all the help I can give – which may not be much. This strike is running us ragged." He nodded politely to us all and left the room.

Lestrade took a sip of his neglected beer. "Well? What do we do now?"

Holmes frowned. "I think it is best that we visit the Geraghty family."

"To let them know you are taking on the case?" I asked.

Holmes nodded. "I have nothing to tell them except that Michael Geraghty's inclinations were correct. There is much more to this murder than a drunken brawl."

"Do you wish me to accompany you?" Lestrade asked.

"If you would be so kind," Holmes replied. "It would be good for the family to know that Scotland Yard is also on the case, even if only in an unofficial capacity."

Lestrade looked thoughtful. "If it becomes apparent to the general public that there has been the miscarriage of justice that there certainly appears to have been, then it will no longer be unofficial." He smiled slightly. "Monro and Anderson take great pride in the reputation of the London Metropolitan Police. I do not believe I will have any great difficulty in persuading them to allow me to reopen the case and request the assistance of Mr. Sherlock Holmes and Doctor John Watson."

"My dear Lestrade," Holmes said delightedly, "You keep revealing depths that are a delight to behold." He looked around the room. "Now, if you have both finished with your drinks, perhaps we could get on to the Geraghtys."

Lestrade took one last sip of his drink, and I pushed mine away untouched, and we got to our feet. We followed Holmes down the stairs, through the bar, and out into the bustling crowds of Spitalfields.

Chapter Five

The footpath was densely packed, with people crushed up close. I kept one hand on my wallet and the other on my watch, and I noticed that Holmes and Lestrade were doing the same.

We threaded our way through the throngs of people. The odour of unwashed bodies, horse manure, and hot sausages from a nearby vendor, made a pungent cocktail of scent as we headed towards Whitechapel High Street.

The address Michael Geraghty had given us proved to be a fine Georgian townhouse, set slightly back from the road, with a path of pretty blue and brown tiles leading from the road to the steps.

A housemaid answered our knock, and when we gave her our names, she conducted us into a front parlour that overlooked Whitechapel High Street, before disappearing into the depths of the house.

The front parlour showed signs of the family's prosperity. Good, solid walnut and mahogany furniture dotted the room. Several pieces of extremely fine French porcelain decorated a sideboard. The centrepiece of the room, however, was a fine painting on one wall of an older man, with a stern expression, dressed in the fashions of the late King George IV when he was Prince Regent.

A voice came from the doorway. "My father-in-law."

I turned towards the voice. An older woman stood in the doorway. Her dark hair was touched with silver and she had warm hazel eyes, much like Michael Geraghty's. I realized that this lady must be his mother.

She came more fully into the room. "I am Winifred Geraghty, gentlemen. The maid told me who you are. Michael isn't here. May I help you? May I hope that you are here about John?"

Holmes bowed over her hand briefly. "That is the reason for our visit, Mrs. Geraghty."

"Please. Take a seat." Mrs. Geraghty waved us towards several comfortable chairs, which we took as the maid wheeled in a tea trolley.

The maid was followed by a young woman with the same brown curly hair, and hazel eyes, of Michael Geraghty and his mother. She was dressed in a pale pink tea gown with small red roses embroidered upon it. Her carriage was erect and her eyes held a firmness of purpose.

Mrs. Geraghty introduced her as her youngest daughter, Julia. Julia seated herself beside her mother, barely acknowledging us with a small murmur, and proceeded to pour the tea and distribute small sandwiches and cakes.

"When will Mr. Geraghty be home?" Holmes asked politely as he sipped his tea.

"He is down at the wharf trying to smooth things down there. I am unsure as to when he will return."

"Have you found who killed John?" Julia demanded.

"Not yet, Miss Geraghty," Holmes replied.

"It was not a drunken brawl," Julia insisted. "No matter what that stupid policeman thought." She was glaring at Lestrade as she spoke.

I closed my eyes briefly. I could see this turning into quite a scene very quickly.

Lestrade, however, surprised me. He carefully placed his cup and saucer down upon a side table and spoke directly to the young woman. "I quite agree, Miss Geraghty. In my mind the investigation into the murder of your brother is one of the shoddiest instances of police work I have seen in my career. That is why I am assisting Mr. Holmes in his investigation."

"That is good news indeed," said Mrs. Geraghty, giving her daughter a quelling look.

"We really do need to speak to Mr. Geraghty," Holmes said. "May we prevail upon someone in your household to show us the way to Duncran Wharf?"

Julia got to her feet. "I will take them, mother."

"And how will you get home safely?" Mrs. Geraghty protested.

"If William is there, he can escort me home; otherwise, I shall wait for Michael and return with him."

"Very well," her mother sighed.

Julia hastened away. Mrs. Geraghty looked at us with a wry smile. "Julia is my youngest. I am afraid she has been overindulged. William will be good for her."

"William?" Holmes asked.

"William Blehane. He is Michael's wharfinger and is courting Julia. A good man, solid, if a little unimaginative."

Julia returned just then; the tea gown swapped for a more appropriate walking dress in a deep blue with matching coat and bonnet, ready to escort us. We made our farewells to Mrs. Geraghty and followed Julia out into Whitechapel High Street.

The walk from the Geraghty residence to Duncran Wharf was not a particularly pleasant one; encompassing as it did many narrow, dark lane ways. I was very much aware of hostile eyes following our every move. I completely understood why Mrs. Geraghty was concerned about Julia walking home alone.

As we got closer to the Thames, I could hear the murmuring of voices, which got louder as we approached. The source turned out to be striking dock workers picketing the London Docks.

It was a sad spectacle indeed. The majority of the men were slender to the point of being emaciated with pinched faces that spoke of chronic malnourishment. The dreadfully low wages paid by the dock owners meant that there was never enough money to properly feed the working men, let alone their wives and children. Hence the ongoing strike.

There were also a few men loitering outside the gates of the more modest Duncran Wharf. One man, a swarthy, surly looking, fellow, began to hurl insults at us. To my consternation, Julia Geraghty marched right up to the picket line and stared him in the eyes.

"You hush your mouth, Jack Tyler. These men are going to find out who killed John. You get out of our way and let us through, or God help me…"

The man, Jack Tyler, backed down immediately. "Steady on, Miss Julia, I don't wanna cop a mouse from you."

"Cop a mouse?" I murmured to Lestrade.

"Get a black eye," Lestrade replied.

Tyler was still talking. "The coves look more like bruisers than rozzers, to me. Especially him." He pointed at me. I glared at him. "But John was a good cove. If that's what they're here for, we ain't gonna interfere, are we lads?" The last was addressed to the rest of the small picket line that had fallen silent during the exchange.

There was much shaking of heads accompanied by murmurs of agreement and the picket line parted like the Red Sea to allow us onto the wharf. We followed Miss Geraghty through the gates and passed a small warehouse until we came to the office that was situated towards the end of the small wharf. The peculiar smell of Thames mud pervaded the air.

Michael Geraghty must have heard the commotion at the gates, as he came out to meet us, accompanied by another man.

This man was a little shorter than Mr. Geraghty, being perhaps five feet, eight inches tall. He had straight black hair, a small straggly moustache, and concerned brown eyes.

"Julia!" the man exclaimed. "What are you doing here?"

"I've brought Mr. Holmes, Doctor Watson and Inspector Lestrade to see Michael. They are going to find John's murderer. And when they do, I shall watch him hang!" Her tone was fierce.

Lestrade opened his mouth, no doubt to point out that there were no public hangings any more, when a nudge from Holmes caused him to close his mouth without speaking.

Michael Geraghty sighed. "Please forgive my sister, gentlemen, she is a little fiery."

The other man chuckled softly. "That she is." He held out his hand for us to shake, a trifle reluctantly, I thought. "William Blehane, gentlemen, at your service."

"Is what Julia says true?" asked Michael Geraghty.

"Yes, Mr. Geraghty, it is," replied Holmes. "By the good offices of Inspector Lestrade here I was able to discern the facts of the case as reported by the police in H. Division."

"Which are?"

"Your brother was most certainly not killed in a drunken brawl. The policeman who handled the case is a fool, and a bigoted fool at that. I am afraid there will probably be little help forthcoming from that direction, even if Inspector Reid is sympathetic."

"But you will hunt for the killer?"

"Certainly, Mr. Geraghty," Holmes assured him. "The good doctor and I, with the able assistance of Inspector Lestrade here, will do our very best to see your brother gets the justice he deserves."

"Thank you, Mr. Holmes. That has taken a great weight from off my mind."

Holmes nodded and then looked around the wharf. "What did your brother do here?"

"John dealt with our importers. Those who brought goods into the country via this wharf. I deal with those who export from our wharf," Michael Geraghty replied. "William here tries to ensure that the entire thing keeps running."

"Which is a little difficult with the strike on. The new Dock, Wharf, Riverside and General Labourers Union is making life difficult for all of us," William commented. "Not helped by the fact that now Jack Tyler is the union's representative on the wharf."

"I believe we met Jack Tyler outside the gates," Holmes commented. "A charming fellow with a limited vocabulary and a rather loud voice."

William snorted. "That's Jack Tyler. Thinks he's cock of the walk now the lads have voted for him to lead them. The sappy idiot couldn't lead a horse to bloody water."

"He could certainly do with learning a few manners," I commented. "His comments when we arrived were extremely uncouth. Especially with a lady present."

William Blehane's countenance darkened. "He was rude to Julia?" He clenched his fists. I suddenly felt apprehensive and wondered if I should have kept my mouth shut.

Lestrade essayed a dry little chuckle. "I shouldn't worry, Mr. Blehane. Tyler seemed quite cowed by Miss Geraghty. He seemed to be afraid of getting a black eye from the lady."

"With good reason," Michael Geraghty commented with a slight smile. "Julia once blacked both of his eyes. Though she was only twelve at the time and Tyler wasn't expecting it."

"A veritable Penthesilea," Lestrade murmured, referencing the Amazonian queen in Homer's Iliad, and giving me a new appreciation of the depth of his knowledge.

"Mr. Geraghty," Holmes said, "When you came to our rooms you said that your brother should have been here that night. What exactly was he supposed to have been doing?"

Michael Geraghty pushed a hand through his hair and sighed. "John was becoming concerned about some discrepancies in the paperwork. He was of the opinion that someone was using our wharf to smuggle illicit goods."

"Such as?" I asked curiously.

"Anything the government charges customs on," Michael Geraghty replied. "Brandy, or the Polish spirit, vodka, for example."

"Did your brother suspect anyone?" Holmes asked.

Michael Geraghty shook his head. "He hadn't got that far. It was suspicions only."

"May I see the papers your brother was working on?"

"Certainly, Mr. Holmes. Do you wish to do it here, or shall I have them delivered to Baker Street?"

"Baker Street, if you please," Holmes said, after a moment's thought. "I find it more congenial to do such work in the confines of my own home."

Michael Geraghty nodded. "I shall have them delivered tonight."

We took our leave of the Geraghtys and William Blehane and walked back down the wharf to the street. As we came out of the gates, Jack Tyler walked towards us. His manner, however, was much different than before.

"You gents are really going to find who did for Johnny Geraghty?"

"If it is at all possible to do so, Mr. Tyler," Holmes replied.

"Peter over there," he waved at a dark-haired fellow who bore more than a passing resemblance to William Blehane, "…tells me you're Sherlock Holmes."

"I am," my friend replied quietly.

"You think you can do better than Bert Woods?"

Lestrade snorted. "A three-year-old child could do better than Sergeant Albert Woods."

Tyler suddenly grinned, showing a mouthful of yellowing teeth. "I like you. You're Lestrade, ain't you? The Scotland Yard Teck."

When Lestrade nodded, he continued. "Anything me or the lads can do to help, just give us a yell. Johnny may have been a boss, but he was a good un. Never turned no-one away, did Johnny. It ain't right that he ended like he did." He stared at us for a moment, nodded to himself, shoved his hands in his pockets and sauntered back to the picket line.

"Well," Holmes murmured. "That was interesting."

We walked away from the wharf in search of a cab that would take us back to Baker Street.

Chapter Six

It was late that evening when Mrs. Hudson ushered William Blehane into our rooms. He carried a rather beaten up Gladstone bag which he handed over to Holmes.

"These were all the papers we could find, Mr. Holmes. Michael thinks that someone has gone through them already. When we went to John's desk we found his papers strewn all over the place. That wasn't like John at all. He was a tidy man. He could not bear clutter."

I noted that Blehane was making a sterling effort not to notice the myriad newspaper cuttings and scribbled notes that had colonized Holmes's desk.

Holmes took the bag from William, and thanked him for his kindness in delivering it. Taking the words for the dismissal it so clearly was, William Blehane wished us a pleasant evening and left our rooms.

I stood at the window and watched him walk away down Baker Street. Behind me, I could hear Holmes rummaging around on his desk as he cleared a space for the bag and its contents.

It was going to be, I reflected, a long night. I turned back to see Holmes carefully removing the papers from the bag and arranging them in piles upon his now cleared desk. I marveled at my friend's ability to clean up so quickly.

A quick look around me showed me that far from cleaning up his other papers, Holmes had merely relocated them onto the floor. I sighed as I stepped over the accumulated detritus of Holmes' previous cases and walked to my chair.

When I retired to bed several hours later, Holmes was still going through John Geraghty's paperwork. His only response to my wishing him a good night, was an absent-minded grunt.

When I arose the next morning, it was to find a deeply disgruntled Holmes slouched at the table eyeing the breakfast eggs as if they were about to commit a major crime.

I took my place and helped myself to the aforementioned eggs, and several rashers of bacon. I waited a few moments before saying "I take it the papers were of no use to you?"

Holmes gave a short bark of humourless laughter. "I congratulate you, my dear doctor, on your growing powers of observation. The papers were of absolutely no use whatsoever. It is clear that the papers are not complete. Some have most definitely been removed. In some instances pages have been quite obviously torn out of journal books."

Holmes scowled at his plate. "I shall need to speak with Michael Geraghty again to find out where their imports come from. That at least will tell me something of what is missing."

I paused with my fork above my plate and gave Holmes a quizzical look. "How so?" I asked.

"According to the papers that remain, goods were brought in from France, Belgium, and Spain. If Michael Geraghty can tell me that goods were also coming in from other countries, then I will at least know where to start looking."

"At the boats from these speculative countries?"

Holmes waved his hand in a rocking motion. "Perhaps yes; perhaps no. According to what papers survive, most of the goods were unloaded at Gravesend and brought up the Thames to Duncran Wharf on lighters. Duncran Wharf being too small to handle the larger vessels that now go to London Docks or St. Katherine Dock."

I thought for a moment. "So the smuggling that John Geraghty suspected was happening could well be at Gravesend rather than London?"

"It is possible," my friend replied, "...but, in my opinion, unlikely."

"Why so?" I asked.

"Someone from Gravesend would be unlikely to have the knowledge of the alleyways around Whitechapel. Nor would John Geraghty be inclined to go down one with someone he barely knew."

"I do not follow," I confessed.

"Think, Watson! John Geraghty was unlikely to see any of the men unloading the larger craft in Gravesend from one year's end to the next. But he would see the workers on Duncran Wharf every day, and the lightermen with almost as much regularity. Such regularity tends to breed trust, even if such trust is not deserved."

Holmes picked up a piece of toast and bit into it. "No, Watson, this murder has its roots deep in London's East End, and that is where we must dig."

It was only a matter of a few hours later that we began to learn just how deep those roots went.

Lestrade appeared in our rooms in a state of some agitation. "I have received a message from Edmund Reid," he said as Mrs. Hudson showed him in.

"What does Inspector Reid want?" Holmes asked.

"Our help," Lestrade replied. "Jack Tyler has been murdered."

Chapter Seven

We left Baker Street in the cab Lestrade had arrived in, and headed towards Whitechapel at a brisk pace. As we travelled along Lestrade said "I came straight from Scotland Yard. Reid sent an official request for assistance. In it he said that he believed that this murder was tied to that of John Geraghty. Anderson showed it to me. Reid asked for me, but he also asked for you, Holmes."

"Anderson acquiesced?" Holmes said with raised brows.

"As much as he doesn't want to admit it," Lestrade said, "He knows damn well that the murders a couple of months ago would not have been solved without you. Scotland Yard owes you. Hell, I owe you my life." Lestrade was referring to the time in that awful case where Holmes's quick actions had saved Lestrade from being bludgeoned to death.

Holmes waved that off with his usual nonchalant air. Thanks, especially the heartfelt variety, always embarrassed him.

"Do we have any details of what happened to Mr. Tyler?" Holmes asked.

Lestrade shook his head. "No. Reid just said that he had been murdered and requested our assistance. We will go to Leman Street, if the cab doesn't get stopped first. Cabs are not common in this part of London. No-one has the money to use them."

"Ah well, we shall discover the details for ourselves soon enough." Holmes sank back into the seat and lapsed into silence.

The cab drew to a halt on Commercial Street. We could hear the cab driver talking with someone. The cabbie opened the roof hatch and looked down at us. "I believe you gents want the murder site?" he asked.

"We do," Holmes replied.

"The peeler here says there's a murder down Dorset Street. Well, I ain't takin' me 'horse an' cab down Dorset. I'll never see bloody either again! So you'll have to jump out here."

We did as we were bid, with Lestrade paying the cabbie, who turned his cab around neatly and trotted briskly back up Commercial Street, as if lingering in Whitechapel could contaminate both man and horse. I had to admit, breathing in the vilely scented air, that the cabman may have had the right of it.

A uniformed constable was talking with Lestrade. "Inspector Reid said you would be coming, sir. The corpse is down here." He pointed to a street leading off Commercial Street.

The street was Dorset Street; a warren of grimy lodging houses and enclosed courts. It was in one of these courts, Miller's Court, that the dreadful remains of Mary Jane Kelly, the final victim of the Whitechapel Murderer, so evocatively called Jack the Ripper by the press, had been discovered.

The Britannia public house stood on the corner of Commercial Street and Dorset Street. Even though it was not yet lunch time, the pub hummed and throbbed with life, much of it antagonistic to the police.

The feeling of encroaching violence ebbed as Edmund Reid came strolling out of Dorset Street. He came striding up to us, holding out his hand. "Thank God you have come, Giles! I am so pleased that Scotland Yard agreed that you could help. I am also pleased to have the assistance of Mr. Sherlock Holmes and Doctor Watson."

I got the feeling that Inspector Reid was putting on a performance for the surrounding listeners. I was aware that Reid was both loved and respected in the East End, and if we were vouched for by him, then we would experience few difficulties and be much less likely to be robbed by the locals.

Inspector Reid led us down Dorset Street to a decrepit lodging house. Most of the lodging houses in this part of the East End were owned by two men. Slum landlords John McCarthy and William Crossingham. Both were well known to the police for a variety of reasons, not all of them savoury.

McCarthy and one of his agents, a man introduced to us as Thomas Bowyer, were waiting for us outside of one of the lodging houses.

McCarthy thumbed over his shoulder to the entrance. "He's in there. Top room. Tom here found him a couple of hours ago when he came to get the rent." His expression grew sour. "Not that he was able to pay. None of the wharfies can."

Reid's face drew into a frown. McCarthy noticed, and the sour expression became a tight smile. "No cause to be looking like that, Inspector. I was giving him tick, like I am all the wharfies.

I looked at Lestrade. He anticipated my question with a tight smile of his own. "Mr. McCarthy was letting him have credit."

McCarthy overheard and shrugged. "If they can't pay now, they'll be able to pay later. If the dock owners give them what they ask, at any road."

Reid nodded and walked into the building, gesturing for us to follow. We made our way up several flights of decidedly rickety stairs to an attic room.

It was hardly a room with a view. The sole source of light being a grubby casement window with cracked glass, and with a view out over the smoke blackened rooftops of Dorset Street and beyond. This had been opened to its fullest extent to allow the meagre light available illuminate to room. It failed. Police bullseye lamps had had to be strategically placed to provide necessary light.

The lamps illuminated a sorry sight. Jack Tyler lay sprawled on his back on top of a dingy bed consisting of a hard straw mattress covered with a rather grubby sheet, and a worn out blanket. Blood soaked the bedding.

The reason for this became clear when Reid grabbed the corpse's shoulder and rolled him enough for us to see the two stab wounds in Jack Tyler's back. Like John Geraghty before him, Jack Tyler had been stabbed in the kidneys. Unlike Geraghty though, Tyler had been placed on his back, allowing him to bleed out.

As I bent to examine the corpse, I noticed Holmes flick his eyes around the room. There was little enough here to provide any clues as to Tyler's murderer.

Apart from the sordid bed, the only other furnishings were a couple of hooks on the wall from which hung a few oddments of old clothing.

Holmes came and stood beside me, looking down at the corpse. "The same as Geraghty, I presume?"

"Based on what Lestrade told us," I replied, "I would say most certainly. Death has been caused by stab wounds to the back which have no doubt severed the renal artery. Though the police surgeon will have to certify that."

"Dr. Phillips has already been," Inspector Reid said. "He was fine with leaving Tyler here until Giles, Mr. Holmes and yourself had inspected the scene."

George Bagster Phillips was the official police surgeon for H. Division and lived locally. He was an amiable, charming man, who endeared himself to the majority of people he met. He had also, along with Dr. Thomas Bond, performed the post-mortem on Mary Jane Kelly. I wondered what he had felt returning to the street where that vile crime had occurred.

Noticing that I was wool-gathering, Holmes nudged me and glared. I turned my attention back to the pitiful remains of Jack Tyler. "There is really nothing else I can tell you about this man's death. Apart from the fact that, like John Geraghty, he obviously trusted his killer."

"Well done, Watson," Holmes murmured. "We will make a detective of you yet."

"If it is all the same to you, Holmes, I will stick to being a doctor and a detective's biographer," I replied.

"He trusted his killer?" Reid asked.

It was Lestrade who answered. "Stabbed in the back in his own lodgings, Edmund."

Reid tilted his head to one side. "I see what you mean. Tyler would not have brought a complete stranger to his room." He paused, and frowned, "Unless it was a whore." Reid shook his head and immediately contradicted himself. "No. Tyler would not have had the money for a whore. Not with the strike being on."

"Given that the most a man like Tyler could expect to earn was around 5d a day, I think he would rarely have had the money for a whore," Lestrade replied.

"Around here, he could have got one for ha'penny, if he wasn't fussy about disease," Reid observed quietly. "But I understand what you are saying."

My mind had caught Inspector Reid's comment on Tyler only earning 5d a day. A room like this would have cost around a shilling, or 12d, a week. I frowned. "5d a day, you say? Surely that's not enough to…" My voice trailed off and I gestured to indicate the room.

"That's what the strike is about, doctor," Inspector Reid replied. "The men are paid 5d per hour to unload the ships. However, they are all so underfed and weak, that they can only work for an hour before exhaustion gets the better of them. So most of them take their 5d and leave. The money buys them a little food, mostly bread and cheese and beer. Not enough to keep their strength up."

I thought of the emaciated men I had seen down at the docks the day before. I had known that the docker's pay was paltry, but not that the sum was quite so meagre.

"The new union wants them to be paid for a minimum of four hours of work, even if they only work one, and to hire workers permanently rather than passing out chits at the gate when each ship comes in." Reid looked down at the body of Jack Tyler. "Jack was an enthusiastic supporter of the new union. Much good that it did him."

"You think the killings are tied into the strike?" Holmes asked, his tone sharp.

"It's possible, Mr. Holmes," Inspector Reid replied, looking away from the corpse. "John Geraghty was from a wharf-owning family. Jack Tyler was the union representative for that wharf. It almost has to be linked."

Holmes snorted. "Not necessarily, Inspector. If I were to walk out into the streets of Whitechapel and ask men where they worked, what replies would I get?"

Inspector Reid gave a rueful smile. "About two-thirds of them would say they worked on or near the river. I take your point, Mr. Holmes." He looked down at Jack Tyler again. "Now what?"

"Now, Inspector, we find out just where Jack Tyler was and who he was with before he returned home to his untimely death."

Inspector Reid turned and headed out of the room. "I will talk to McCarthy and Bowyer. They may have known Tyler's routine. I certainly don't. That is one thing about Tyler. He wasn't a trouble maker. We were never called to brawls that he was involved in."

"Tyler may not have been a trouble maker," Lestrade observed quietly. "But trouble certainly found him."

Chapter Eight

We left the remains of Jack Tyler to be taken to the morgue, and followed Inspector Reid down the stairs and out into the squalor and bustle of Whitechapel.

Thomas Bowyer was still waiting at the bottom of the stairs. John McCarthy was nowhere to be seen. Bowyer fidgeted nervously from foot to foot, as if the cobblestones beneath his feet were red hot. "The boss said to tell you he had to get back to work, but I was to tell what I saw."

Reid raised an eyebrow at him. "What did you see?"

Bowyer waved a hand towards the upstairs room where Jack Tyler lay. "I saw him. Tyler. Last night."

"Where?" Holmes asked.

"Outside the soup kitchen. The big one on Cable Street. Don't know if he was going in or coming out. He was near it, anyway."

"Thank you, Tom," Inspector Reid said. "You've been most helpful. Tell McCarthy that I appreciate it."

Tom Bowyer grinned at Inspector Reid. "Just catch the bugger what did for him, Mr. Reid. The boss reckons murder is bad for business." With that the man scampered up Dorset Street and rapidly disappeared from view.

"Soup kitchen on Cable Street?" Lestrade asked Reid.

Reid nodded. "It's the largest one in the area. It's in the Mahogany Bar Mission."

Lestrade frowned, as if trying to place it.

Holmes smiled slightly. "I believe it was once a music hall, Lestrade, and also a pub, hence the name Mahogany Bar. It was purchased by the Methodist Church about twelve years ago and made the centre of their mission in the East End."

Inspector Reid nodded. "Between them and the Booths' Salvation Army, the strikers and their families are being kept well fed. Indeed, most of them are better fed now than at any other time in their lives."

"Which is a sad commentary on life in the East End of this fair city," Holmes said drily. "Now, Inspector Reid, pray lead the way. I think we need to discover who at the soup kitchen saw Jack Tyler."

We walked away from Dorset Street and into the pulsing heart of London's East End. Inspector Reid led us down a maze of narrow dingy streets and lanes until we emerged onto Cable Street. Most of the people we had passed had looked at us sullenly, but none were overtly hostile.

I noted several Salvationists handing out bread and also meal tickets for the Salvation Army's soup kitchens and for local shops where they could be exchanged for goods. William and Catherine Booth had done good work in London's East End. Their three S's: soup, soap, and salvation, had proven to be a godsend to many of the district's poorer residents, of which there were thousands.

The Mahogany Bar Mission on Cable Street was a huge, somewhat shabby, hall. The building had been modelled upon the more successful upmarket music halls such as the Canterbury Hall in Lambeth and the Royal Holborn. It dominated Grace Alley, where it sat overlooking Cable Street, like a down-at-the-heels dowager. At its peak of popularity, the hall could easily accommodate fifteen hundred people, both seated on benches and standing around the walls. Now, in the hands of the Methodist church, it was performing quite a different function.

At the moment it was providing over a thousand meals a day to starving dock labourers and their families. At other times it fed and sheltered anyone who needed help. For the Methodists did not care what the beliefs or backgrounds of those who sought their help were. Londoner or lascar – either would find the aid they so desperately needed.

A couple of uniform constables were standing watch outside on the opposite side of the street. We went across to talk to them. Reid asked them about Jack Tyler.

"He usually comes here for a meal every day," one of the constables said.

"Not just for the food," the other one added. "But to keep an eye on the strikers. He's afraid they'll give in and go back to work."

The other snorted derisively. "Not likely. They're all eating better from the mission than they do when they're working."

Reid thanked them, and we crossed the road and walked up to the entrance to the hall.

A well-dressed young man stood just inside the door. He raised his eyebrows as we entered the building. "May I help you gentlemen? If you don't mind my saying so, you don't look like you need food from us."

"We don't," Reid said with a slight smile. "I am Inspector Reid from H. Division. This is Inspector Lestrade from Scotland Yard, Mr. Sherlock Holmes, and Doctor John Watson. Might we have a word with whoever is in charge?"

The young man's eyes widened. "Notable visitors indeed. I will take you to meet Mrs. Morgan. She is in charge here today."

He signaled to another man to watch the door and led us into the hall. Galleries ran along the top of the hall leading towards a raised stage surmounted by a fine proscenium arch.

Near the stage massive tables had been set up, and behind them well dressed women, with crisp, starched, white aprons, were busily serving food to the people waiting in line with quiet patience. As the people were served, they took their meal and headed to tables that had been laid out in orderly rows in the middle of the hall.

When people finished eating, they took their crockery and cutlery to tables near the door, where other volunteers washed them in tubs of hot soapy water and carefully dried them before carrying them back up the hall to be used again. It was neat, smooth, and orderly, and I could not help but be impressed by the way it flowed.

Her Majesty's army could not have managed anything quite so well. I said so. The young man leading us up the hall laughed. "I shall certainly tell Mrs. Morgan that, Doctor Watson. She will be delighted with the praise."

A middle-aged woman with dark hair, sharp blue eyes, and a no-nonsense attitude saw us coming up the hall and stepped away from where she was serving and came to meet us.

"Simon? Who are these people?" Her tone was not welcoming. No doubt she took us for newspaper people. There had been a lot of coverage of the strike in London's papers, much of it hysterical and vituperative although there had been some support for the plight of the dock workers and their families. This was especially true once reports of the dire poverty and exploitation of the dock labourers had become public knowledge.

"Mrs. Morgan, this is Inspector Reid, Inspector Lestrade, Mr. Sherlock Holmes, and Doctor John Watson. They wished to speak with the person in charge."

"Indeed? And what brings such eminent gentlemen to a soup kitchen in the East End?"

"Murder, dear lady," Holmes replied softly. "What else?"

"No-one has been murdered here, Mr. Holmes," Mrs. Morgan replied firmly.

I felt it was highly unlikely that anyone would even attempt murder under the nose of so formidable a lady as Mrs. Morgan.

"Indeed not," Holmes replied. "But a man who was here last night has been."

The lady looked at Holmes, her head tilted to one side. "And you wish to speak with whoever was here and may have seen him?"

"That is correct. You have a keen grasp of the situation, ma'am." Holmes replied.

"None of my female volunteers were here last night. It is not safe for an unaccompanied woman to be on the streets in this part of London at night." She looked at Simon. "Go around the tables, ask who was here last night and saw…" She paused, and gave us an inquiring look.

Holmes gave a polite smile, understanding what she was silently asking. "Jack Tyler," he said.

Mrs. Morgan looked back at Simon, "Ask if anyone saw Jack Tyler here last night."

He nodded and strode off towards the tables.

Mrs. Morgan escorted us back down the hall towards the entrance. "Forgive me gentlemen, but I would prefer it if you waited here. I do not want this place in an uproar."

"We quite understand," Holmes assured her.

She left us near the door and headed back up the hall to the serving tables. I looked around the room. A young, dark-haired woman was carrying a pile of freshly scrubbed plates up the hall. When she turned to come back down the hall, I blinked with astonishment. It was Dorothy Watts.

Dorothy, born Daniel, was a brave young he/she lady who had been instrumental in stopping a vicious killer a couple of months previously. She had been the ward, for want of a better term, of Sir Lucas Catterick, 5th Baronet Undershaw. At the conclusion of the case, the Catterick household had moved to France, but Dorothy had remained behind in London, going to work for Mycroft Holmes. I wondered what her presence here presaged.

I turned towards Holmes, eager to share my discovery. I did not get the chance.

"I spotted her the moment we entered, Watson," Holmes said with some amusement. "Interesting that she should be here at this time, is it not?"

"Who?" Inspector Reid asked curiously.

"A young lady of our acquaintance," Lestrade said. "Miss Watts."

"The dark haired, doe-eyed lass?" Reid asked.

We all nodded.

Reid watched Dorothy with some interest. "An acquaintance of yours, you say? I know that it is becoming fashionable for women to become private detectives, but she's a little young for the profession, don't you think?"

"An interesting piece of deduction, Inspector," Holmes said drily. "Not entirely accurate, but interesting all the same."

We were saved from having to elaborate by the arrival of Simon with a sullen, unshaven, man in tow. He introduced his surly companion as Robert Glasheen.

"Robert works, sorry, worked with Jack on Duncran Wharf."

"Thank you. You have been most helpful," said Reid.

Simon nodded and left us to talk to Robert Glasheen. The man glowered at us, obviously not inclined to talk to us at all. In an unspoken agreement, we let Inspector Reid take charge.

"Robert, did Simon tell you why we want to speak to you?"

"Aye. Some rawmaish about Jack being murdered."

"It's not nonsense," Inspector Reid said sharply, "We've just come from his lodgings where his corpse lays stiffening in its own blood upon the bed."

Glasheen snorted. "Old McCarthy won't like that. He'll have to replace the bedding before he can let that rat-infested hovel he calls a room."

"I take it you are familiar with Jack Tyler's lodgings," said Lestrade.

Glasheen just looked at him. "McCarthy's lodgings are all the same. Been in one and you've been in them all. Not a one of them is fit for man or beast."

"You have better accommodation?" Lestrade asked, eyebrows raised in quiet disbelief.

"Robert here still lives with his family, don't you Robbie, lad?" Reid said softly. "They're a little better off than many of the others. Glasheen senior runs a little shop in Wapping."

"So why are you eating here, if your family is better off than most?" Lestrade asked.

Robert Glasheen shot him a look full of dislike. "The strike's making it hard for everyone. Me dad's making very little in the shop. He's accepting the meal tickets that the do-gooders are giving out, but it's a bugger trying to get the money out of the do-gooders when you present the tickets to them. Them what supplies the shop won't take meal tickets. It's better for everyone if I eat here. Less strain on the family."

Lestrade nodded, satisfied with his response.

Robert Glasheen looked around at the four of us. "Jack Tyler really is dead?"

"He really is dead, Robbie," Inspector Reid said softly. "You know me. Would I joke about that?"

Glasheen scratched awkwardly at the back of his head. "Reckon you wouldn't, Mr. Reid." He examined the floor as if searching for inspiration. Finally, he looked up at us. "I saw Jack last night. He ate here. We had a really good vegetable soup with lots of fresh bread, and tea. We talked for a bit about how the strike was going. Him, me, Peter, Michael, Martin and the other Rob."

"Peter, Michael, Martin, and the other Rob?" Holmes asked.

"Peter Blehane, Michael Fennessy, Martin Pennefather, and Rob Hoban. We all work on Duncran Wharf."

"Is Peter Blehane related to William?" asked Lestrade.

Glasheen nodded. "William is Peter's older brother."

"Are the others here?" Lestrade asked.

Glasheen shook his head. "Martin, Michael and Rob were here earlier. Peter will be along later. He doesn't come for food. The Blehanes have enough. They mostly eat with the boss's family, seeing as William be courting the youngest Geraghty colleen. Peter comes to encourage the men to continue with the strike. They're getting pretty down on it."

Inspector Reid nodded. "The dock owners hope that if they hold out long enough you will have to give in."

"Ain't going to happen," Robert Glasheen said firmly.

"Jack Tyler?" Holmes asked, getting impatient with what I could tell he thought was unnecessary chit chat.

"I saw him last night. Outside the hall. He was talking with a cove."

"Did you recognize the man?" Reid asked.

Glasheen nodded. "I did. It was James Harrison."

"James Harrison?" Lestrade asked.

"Works for London Docks," Reid replied.

"Aye," said Glasheen, "And a right little bastard he is. Always pushing for the boss to sell Duncran to London Docks. I heard him threaten the boss once."

"I bet that did not go down too well," Lestrade commented.

Glasheen grinned, a vicious, feral sort of a grin. "It didn't. Boss threatened to cart him down to the end o' the wharf and chuck him in the Thames. Harrison scarpered pretty sharpish after that. Ain't been back to Duncran Wharf since."

"I wonder why," Holmes observed sardonically.

Glasheen laughed at Holmes's remark and took his leave of us, heading back to the table and his now cooling food.

We paused at the door to thank Simon for his help, then exited out into Grace Alley and up onto Cable Street.

"So?" said, Lestrade. "What now?"

"I think a visit to Mr. Harrison at the London Docks would be advisable," replied Holmes.

As we turned to head in the direction of the docks, we heard the sound of someone running, and then a voice gasped out Inspector Reid's name.

We turned and saw a breathless young constable come panting up to us.

"Good Lord, Sims, what on earth is the matter?" asked Inspector Reid.

The young constable, Sims, stood for a moment, bent over with his hands on his thighs gasping for breath. Running in the polluted air of London was never a good idea at the best of times.

Constable Sims straightened up and looked at Inspector Reid. "We found something, sir, when the body was being shifted. It fell out of his trouser leg. Sergeant Leeson reckoned it must've been stitched to the waistband of his trousers and when he was stabbed it was cut loose."

"What was cut loose?" Inspector Reid asked with a great deal of patience.

"This." Constable Sims dug a package wrapped in a piece of grubby oilskin out of his tunic and handed it to Inspector Reid.

Cautiously, Reid peeled back the edge of the cloth. We all gaped in astonishment when a large wad of bank notes was revealed.

Chapter Nine

We went post haste to Reid's office at the Whitechapel Police Station in Leman Street. There the package was unwrapped completely and the money counted. To our consternation the package contained around one hundred pounds in used notes. Such a sum as the average man was unlikely to see in six months. For a man such as Tyler, the amount was impossible for him to have obtained legally.

Lestrade gazed gloomily at the money sitting on Reid's desk. "Well, it looks like John Geraghty was right about someone smuggling through Duncran Wharf. Maybe Geraghty found out that Tyler was involved. Could Tyler be Geraghty's killer?"

Holmes snorted. "Oh yes, of course, Lestrade. Then Tyler, in a fit of remorse, stabbed himself in the back. Twice! Really, Lestrade. You know better than that!"

Lestrade glared at Holmes for a moment, then his face took on a rueful expression. "You have a point," he conceded. "Although Tyler obviously knew whoever killed Geraghty."

"And was most likely involved in the supposed smuggling," said Reid, supporting his Scotland Yard colleague.

"Maybe yes; maybe no," replied Holmes. "We can surmise that Tyler was involved in smuggling, but we have no proof that he was. This money may well have come from another, equally illegal, endeavour."

"So what now?" I asked.

"Now, my dear Watson, we take a refreshing stroll down to London Docks are see if Mr. James Harrison is as interested in talking to us as he was to talk with the late Mr. Tyler."

When we left Leman Street, Inspector Reid was making arrangements for the money to be transported to Scotland Yard for safe-keeping. He was not sanguine about the honesty of too many of Whitechapel's residents who passed through the station's halls.

"They've nicked tea, sugar, and bread," Reid said sourly, "and they'd steal the furniture if they could work out how to get it out of the station without being seen. Let's not give them opportunity to have it away with that amount of cash."

Leaving Reid to his arrangements, Holmes, Lestrade and I walked down Leman Street and turned towards the Thames.

The London Docks, or, more accurately, the London and St. Katherine's Docks, as they had merged together some ten years or so previously, dominated the Thames.

The dock complex could hold almost four hundred ships at one time, and it contained a mass of enormous warehouses. One of the largest, measuring seven hundred and fifty two feet long by one hundred and sixty feet wide, was used to store tobacco. It was interesting to muse on the fact that both the tobacco that Holmes and I used in our pipes, and that which was made into the cigarettes Holmes occasionally smoked, had all come through this impressive port.

As we approached the gates of the docks, we could hear shouting. Getting closer we realized why. It was a picket line of strikers, and, given the size of the docks, a much larger one than that which had impeded the gates to Duncran Wharf.

Ragged, angry, men were shouting slogans and demands at the gates, which were guarded on the inside by several indifferent men whose only qualifications for the job appeared to be their size.

The picket line turned its attention on us as we approached. I was afraid that we would be mistaken for dock management and attacked. Whilst I am no coward, the thought of taking on at least a hundred men, did not strike me as having particularly good odds of us coming out alive.

Lestrade surprised me by stopping, turning towards the men and holding his hand up for silence. After a chorus of abusive shouts and catcalls, the men quietened down.

Lestrade raised his voice so he could be heard clearly. "We are not dock management, lads. You've all heard about the murder of John Geraghty and now Jack Tyler?"

There was a mumbled sound of agreement and some nodding of heads.

"I am Inspector Lestrade from Scotland Yard, and this is Mr. Sherlock Holmes and Doctor John Watson. We are investigating their murders."

"What's wrong with Eddy Reid, then?" a voice shouted. "He not good enough?"

"Edmund Reid is a bloody good detective," Lestrade yelled back. "But you fellows are enough for him to handle at the moment. So he asked for our help."

Good-natured laughter greeted Lestrade's words, and the picket-line slid backwards to allow us to approach the gate.

"Well done, Lestrade," Holmes murmured sotto voce.

"Well done, indeed," I agreed. "I was not looking forward to facing off against so many."

Lestrade shrugged off our praise as we got closer to the gates. "If you want to survive as a copper on London's streets, you learn to think fast and talk even faster."

One of the hard-eyed bruisers manning the entrance glared at us. "What do you want?"

"To talk to Mr. James Harrison."

"Maybe 'e don't wanna talk to you."

"Let him be the judge of that," Lestrade snapped.

The guard bristled. Holmes stepped up to the gate. "Now then, Jacky Roundhouse, none of that."

The bruiser squinted at Holmes. "Oh blimey! It is you, Mr. 'Olmes. Didn't recognize you for a second. Won't be a tick." He signaled to one of the other guards, and they opened the gates just enough to let us squeeze through.

The guard that Holmes had called Jacky Roundhouse gave Lestrade an apologetic look. "Sorry for all that, Inspector. It's just we've had 'em trying to get onto the docks to cause damage."

"I am fairly sure that none of them posed as Scotland Yard detectives or consulting detectives," Lestrade said.

"You'd be surprised," Roundhouse said, with a lopsided grin that showed that he was missing several teeth. He looked at Holmes. "When you coming back to fight, Mr. 'Olmes? I miss facing off against yer in the ring."

"Perhaps one day I will, Jacky," Holmes replied. "But at the moment, I am a trifle busy. I am sure you understand."

The big man nodded. "Yer a bloody good fighter, Mr. 'Olmes. "At least I've managed to keep me teeth against the others."

I looked at the imposing physique of the guard, and Holmes's sturdy, but wiry frame. Holmes saw my look and chuckled drily. "I got in a fortunate punch, Watson. I doubt I would have lasted long against Jacky if the fight had gone on many more rounds."

"Don't understate yourself, Mr. 'Olmes," Jacky said, shaking his head. "You're a bonny fighter, that you are. You got speed and skill. That will always outmatch brawn like mine."

"Good of you to say so, Jacky, but I think we must agree to disagree on that particular subject," Holmes said. "Now, Mr. James Harrison, if you please."

Grinning, Jacky pointed out a large building about halfway down the docks. "Mr. 'Arrison has an office in there. 'E should be in there. Saw 'im come in this morning and I ain't seen 'im leave."

Thanking the man for his help, we walked down the dock in the direction of the building indicated.

"Unusual name," Lestrade commented.

"What is?" I asked.

"That fellow at the gates. Roundhouse."

"It is a nickname he got while fighting," Holmes explained. "He really only has one decent punch in his repertoire, and that is the roundhouse. His real name is Jack Miller, but he has been known as Jacky Roundhouse by followers of the fancy for years. I doubt many people even know his real name any more."

"He appeared to be a little punch-drunk," I commented. "It is entirely possible that even he does not remember his own name."

A man of middle years, dressed like a clerk, came down the docks towards us. "May I help you gentlemen?"

"We would like to speak with Mr. James Harrison, if he is available," said Lestrade. "I am Inspector Lestrade of Scotland Yard, and this is Mr. Sherlock Holmes and Doctor John Watson."

The fellow gave no sign that he recognized our names. He merely nodded and said, "If you come with me, gentlemen, I shall take you to Mr. Harrison."

The man, who did not introduce himself, took us into the building that Jacky Roundhouse had pointed out to us.

We were left standing in a bare room, while our escort disappeared up a flight of stairs. He returned shortly with another man in tow.

This man was younger, considerably better dressed, and came up to us holding out his hand for us to shake. He peered at us with watery pale blue eyes.

"Peters here told me you wished to see me. I am James Harrison. What can I do for you gentlemen?"

"Is there somewhere we may speak privately?" Lestrade asked.

"In my office," Harrison replied and led us up the stair to a small office with one small window that let in very little light, lending the room a gloomy aspect. The reason for Harrison's watery eyes became clear.

Harrison sat behind his desk. There were no other chairs in the room, and Harrison did not offer to fetch any. He clearly knew who we were and why we were here and wanted us gone as soon as possible, even if it meant being obviously rude.

"Now, gentlemen, what do you want?"

"Tell us what you know about Jack Tyler," Lestrade said.

"Jack Tyler?" Harrison shook his head. "I do not know anyone of that name."

"You were seen talking with him quite amiably last night outside the soup kitchen in Cable Street," I commented.

Harrison shrugged. "I no doubt spoke to someone. Perhaps even gave them a little money. Times are hard, you know."

"Mr. Harrison," Lestrade said coldly, "Do not take us for fools. Your employers want the strike over and the men back earning the pittance they deign to pay them. That you would be giving a striker money of out the goodness of your heart beggars belief."

"There is also the fact," Holmes, who had been silent until now, put in, "…that your employers wish to purchase Duncran Wharf."

"What has that to do with anything?" Harrison asked.

"Jack Tyler was found dead this morning. He had on his person a large sum of money. I do wonder where he got that money from."

"You think I gave him the money?" Harrison's eyes were bulging in his outrage. For a moment I thought he was going to have an apoplectic attack.

"Someone gave him the money," Holmes said softly. "And for no good reason, I am sure. If Duncran Wharf were to go broke under the weight of this strike the London and St. Katherine's Docks Company would be only too pleased to take it off the Geraghty family's hands. It would be worth it for them to keep the wharf's men on strike, but they would need an inside man to do it."

"There is also the matter of the murder of John Geraghty," Lestrade added.

"You think I am responsible for *two* murders?" Harrison's eyes blazed with fury. "I refuse to answer your ridiculous accusations. Get out of my office, or I shall have you thrown out!"

Holmes gestured for us to proceed him out of the door. In the doorway he turned back to Harrison. "A word of advice,

Mr. Harrison. You are swimming in dangerous waters. The men you are in debt to do not play nice. Michael Geraghty merely threatened to throw you into the Thames. You could well have survived that. You will not survive them."

James Harrison was gaping at him like a stunned fish as Holmes closed the door and followed us down the stairs.

Nothing was said until we had left the docks behind us and were walking back to where we would more easily obtain a cab.

"Holmes," I asked. "Do you really think Harrison is the murderer?"

Holmes shook his head. "It is possible, but unlikely. For a start I cannot imagine either Geraghty or Tyler trusting him enough to turn their backs on him." He paused, "There is also the fact that he man does not appear to have the nerve for such a thing. Both killings were risky. John Geraghty was stabbed close by a busy public house, and Jack Tyler in a crowded lodging house. Our killer has an iron nerve."

"Harrison certainly doesn't have that," Lestrade observed. "He was as twitchy as a rabbit in a lettuce patch."

A thought struck me. "Holmes," I said, "How did you know Harrison was in debt?"

"There were several things, Watson, that made that quite obvious."

I looked at Lestrade, who shrugged, obviously as perplexed as I was.

"They were not obvious to us, Holmes," I said.

"When we first arrived, Harrison was polite and inclined to be helpful."

"Yes. So?" said Lestrade.

"The moment he realized that we were there about Jack Tyler's murder his attitude changed."

"But Holmes," I cried. "His attitude was unpleasant from the start. He never offered to get chairs for us."

Holmes shook his head. "That was fear, Watson. He wanted us gone. To say our piece and leave. Harrison thought we were there to menace him on behalf of the betting gang he is in the clutches of."

Lestrade's moustache twitched irritably. "I did introduce myself as a policeman."

"You know as well as I do, Lestrade, that policemen can be bought. This gang has more than one detective on their payroll. It is not a great stretch of the imagination to believe that they could also employ a consulting detective and his associate."

Lestrade inclined his head with a slight scowl, acknowledging Holmes's words whilst not being entirely happy with them.

"How do you know Harrison is in debt to a betting ring?" I asked.

"There were several things, my dear Watson, that pointed to that conclusion."

I sighed. "I did not see them, and neither did Lestrade, so pray enlighten us, Holmes."

"Of course, my dear fellow. In the first instance there were Harrison's cufflinks."

"His cufflinks?" Lestrade asked.

Holmes nodded. "Harrison is well dressed. His suit fairly new and reasonably expensive. What you would expect for a man in his position. His cufflinks, however, were much cheaper. I would have expected to see them on a junior clerk's wrists. By themselves, however, they meant nothing, but combined with the watch chain…"

"Watch chain?" I exchanged a baffled look with Lestrade.

"Harrison was wearing a watch chain across his waistcoat, but there was no watch attached."

"How could you tell?" asked Lestrade.

"Look at yourselves. You both have watch chains across the front of your waistcoats."

We dutifully looked down at ourselves.

"You also each have a slight bulge where your watch is resting in your fob pocket. Harrison did not have such a bulge. Therefore he was wearing a watch chain but no watch. Where was the watch? I will tell you. It is in the same place as his good cufflinks. In a pawn shop."

"I follow that," Lestrade said, after a moment. "...but the betting ring?"

"There were two pieces of paper poking out from the edge of the blotter on Harrison's desk," Holmes replied. "One was clearly a pawnbroker's ticket. They are most distinctive. The other was a betting slip. I recognized it as one issued by one of London's more notorious criminal gangs. This particular gang makes most of its money from extortion, but they have a lucrative sideline in betting on the horses. I suspect that Mr. James Harrison owes them a great deal more money than pawning his cufflinks and watch will provide."

"And Jack Tyler?" Lestrade said.

Holmes shook his head. "We will probably never be able to prove it, but I suspect that the money found on him came from the London and St Katherine's Docks Company. A hundred pounds to one man to keep a strike going until the owners are bankrupt is a mere drop in the ocean compared to what they will make if they can incorporate Duncran Wharf into their holdings."

I made some incoherent spluttering noises.

Holmes looked at me. "It is unscrupulous, Watson, but not illegal."

"Mores the pity," Lestrade observed morosely.

Chapter Ten

We parted ways with Lestrade heading back to Leman Street to tell Reid what we had, or rather had not, discovered. Holmes and I caught a cab and returned to Baker Street.

Holmes caught me by surprise when, upon entering the house, he called loudly for Mrs. Hudson.

That good lady came bustling out of the kitchen wiping her hands upon a cloth as she did so.

"Why the ruckus, Mr. Holmes?" she asked, somewhat tartly. It was clear from the flour upon her apron that she had been baking and did not appreciate being called away from it by her importunate tenant.

"We will be having a visitor, Mrs. Hudson," Holmes said. "I was wondering if, perhaps, we could have some of your delicious scones." He sniffed the air. "…and perhaps a slice or two of that apple cake that I can smell baking?"

Mrs. Hudson smiled. "I think I can manage that. At what time are you expecting your visitor?"

"No later than six o'clock, I believe," Holmes replied.

"I shall keep it light then, so as to leave room for your supper. You are eating in?"

"Yes, Mrs. Hudson. Though we may have to go out later." Holmes headed for the stairs, then turned back. "Is there enough mutton stew to feed Lestrade as well?"

"Mr. Holmes, there is enough mutton stew to feed the entirety of Scotland Yard," Mrs. Hudson replied.

"Excellent! If you could send a telegram to the Yard asking Lestrade to be here by seven, I would be much obliged." He turned again and went up the stairs.

Mrs. Hudson dispatched Billy to send the telegram and I walked upstairs to our rooms.

I entered to find Holmes seated in his chair filling his pipe with tobacco from his Persian slipper.

I sat down in my chair opposite him, frowning slightly. "Holmes…"

"Yes, Watson?"

"What visitor and how do you know the time this person will arrive?"

Holmes put the slipper back on the mantelpiece, lit his pipe, and sat back, puffing contentedly for a few moments.

"It really should be glaringly obvious, Watson, if you think about it."

I thought about it for a while. Holmes was inviting Lestrade to dine with us, but not until after our mysterious visitor had been. I could not see who the visitor could be except for… I looked up at Holmes. "You are expecting Dorothy to call?"

"Well done, Watson!" Holmes beamed.

"But why no later than six o'clock?"

"When Miss Watts completes her shift at the soup kitchen, she will, most naturally, report our visit to Mycroft. She will do this at his office in Whitehall, rather than at the Diogenes Club. Our Miss Watts would tend to stand out a little too much at the Diogenes. She will come from there to here. Given the time it takes to get from Whitechapel to Whitehall, and from Whitehall to Marylebone, I am expecting her to arrive a little before six o'clock."

"But to what purpose?"

"No doubt to issue an invitation, or rather a summons, to see Mycroft."

"But why is Mycroft interested in a soup kitchen?" I asked.

"It is not the soup kitchen, Doctor Watson," a pleasant contralto voice said from the doorway, "…but what is going on in there and at the docks."

We both looked towards the door to see Dorothy Watts standing there, a gentle smile on her face. She was dressed in an expensive suit comprising a divided skirt of the sort much loved by the Rational Dress Society, and close fitting jacket. Both in well-tailored dark blue linen. A matching hat completed the ensemble.

Dorothy looked every inch the sort of community-minded young woman who would lend her time to good works such as the Cable Street soup kitchen.

Holmes got to his feet, and ushered her to the other chair. I glanced at the clock on the mantelpiece. It showed that the time was a quarter past five. Quite a bit before six o'clock.

Holmes caught my glance and chuckled drily. "I did say before six o'clock. Private carriage?" The question was addressed to Dorothy.

Dorothy seated herself, arranging her skirts decorously around her. "Yes, Mr. Holmes. Your brother felt it was more in keeping with the story I am using at the soup kitchen, than using a cab would be."

Holmes looked at me. "I calculated the time based on the use of a cab. A private carriage, of course, has no waiting time."

"Of course," I replied drily. Carriage or cab, it mattered not, Holmes' calculation of who was coming and when was still impressive.

Mrs. Hudson entered then, with a tray with a pot of tea, cups, milk, sugar, some of her apple cake, still steaming from the oven, and a plate of scones with accompanying pots of jam and cream. Holmes, who was still standing, took the tray from her and set it upon the table.

When Mrs. Hudson had poured us all tea and left, Holmes retook his seat, eyeing Dorothy keenly.

"Private carriage?" he asked again.

Dorothy nodded. "To the good people at the Mission I am a young woman of means with the wherewithal to hire a carriage rather than a cab, looking to help where I can. The carriage is one that your brother has at his disposal. The driver is also in your brother's employ, so I am safe to go where I need to."

Holmes nodded. "Mycroft thinks of everything."

"Do you like working for him?" I asked.

Dorothy smiled at me brightly. "It is certainly a great deal different to being a clerk. And certainly different from being Lady Caroline's companion. I find that I am enjoying it. It is interesting, and, at times, exciting, and I am doing something far more useful than I was before."

"Where are you lodging?" I asked, remembering the house in Cleveland Street, and later Sir Lucas Catterick's house in Kensington.

"I have rooms with a widow in Putney. You may remember her? Mrs. Bradstreet."

Holmes chuckled drily and without humour. "It seems Mycroft took my advice most thoroughly."

During the case I had called the Molly-Boy Murders, we had encountered a number of intelligent women, and Holmes had recommended, somewhat sarcastically I must admit, that Mycroft should consider hiring women for his secret work.

Viola Bradstreet was the widow of one of Mycroft's agents and had proved to be a woman with a sharp and intelligent mind, following Holmes's train of thought almost effortlessly.

"Indeed, Mr. Holmes," Dorothy said. "Mrs. Bradstreet is well aware of who and what I am and your brother has had proof of her discretion. He approached her about the possibility of her renting out rooms and she leaped at the chance. I think she is rather bored, to be honest." Dorothy placed her cup upon the side table, "As to why I am here, your brother requests your presence at the Diogenes Club tomorrow evening."

Holmes raised his eyebrows. "Tomorrow evening?"

Dorothy smiled, a cheeky somewhat gamin smile, "Yes, Mr. Holmes. I believe your brother wishes to check a few points with other agents before he speaks with you."

Holmes nodded.

Dorothy rose gracefully to her feet and moved towards the door. She paused and looked back over her shoulder, "I almost forgot. Your brother would like you to bring Inspector Lestrade with you, seeing as he appears to be involved in your business in Whitechapel."

"He will be with us," I assured her.

"What time?" Holmes asked.

"Six o'clock tomorrow evening," came the reply.

Dorothy smiled and took her leave. Holmes watched her go and turned to me with a slight smile. "Well, Watson, whatever else came out of that infernal case, we can be well pleased with that particular outcome."

"Indeed, Holmes," I replied, returning his smile. "That is a person clearly comfortable with themselves. Mycroft did Dorothy a good turn when he took her on as an agent."

Holmes snorted gently. "He did himself a better one. Dorothy is a competent and dangerous young woman, as you are well aware."

I winced as my mind returned to that cold and foggy night at Westminster Bridge where if it had not been for Dorothy's quick actions I could well have lost my life.

Holmes noted my response and said, "I did not mean that in a harsh manner, my friend. I simply meant that we have both seen her in action and know what she is capable of."

"And Mycroft was impressed with the results."

"He was indeed, and so he should have been," Holmes replied. With that he picked up one of the day's newspapers and engrossed himself in that, leaving me to pack the tea things onto a tray and take them down to Mrs. Hudson.

Chapter Eleven

Lestrade arrived promptly at 7 o'clock and was ushered into our rooms by Mrs. Hudson; that good lady smiling, as she always did at Lestrade's fulsome compliments.

Lestrade removed his hat and coat and joined us at table. Mrs. Hudson returned with a tureen of her excellent mutton stew with dumplings, accompanied by mashed potatoes and bread and butter.

There was little in the way of conversation as we applied our attentions to Mrs. Hudson's cooking. While not a marvelous cook, Mrs. Hudson's meals were always solid and satisfying.

When the last of the gravy had been wiped from the plate with the last of the bread, Lestrade sat back in his chair with a sigh of contentment. He exuded an air of good will as he beamed at as. "Thank you for the excellent dinner, gentlemen."

Holmes waved a hand, "Do not thank us. Mrs. Hudson did the cooking. Thank her."

That aforementioned lady, who had entered to clear the table, smiled, "The Inspector already has, Mr. Holmes. Such lovely flowers he brought me."

Holmes and I turned our attention on Lestrade, eyebrows raised in mutual amusement. Lestrade scowled at us. When Mrs. Hudson had left the room he cleared his throat. "What? My mother raised me properly. That is all."

"Of course she did," I said with dry amusement.

"No-one could ever accuse you of being less than a gentleman, Lestrade," Holmes added with equal dryness.

"Did you gentlemen invite me to dinner for a reason, or merely to have fun at my expense?" Lestrade enquired with some amusement of his own.

"There is always a reason, Lestrade," Holmes said. "We had a visitor earlier this evening bearing an invitation."

"Who was the visitor and what was the invitation?"

"The visitor was Miss Watts and the invitation was to call upon Mycroft at the Diogenes Club tomorrow evening," replied Holmes.

Lestrade nodded slowly, as if the information confirmed something that he had suspected. "We are to learn from the horse's mouth exactly what Dorothy is investigating at the soup kitchen, I take it."

"Very much so."

"And your brother no doubt wishes to know why we were in Whitechapel today."

"My dear Lestrade, I suspect Mycroft knew that thirty minutes after we left the district."

"That long?" I queried.

"It would take that long for one of his informants to reach Whitehall," Holmes replied.

Lestrade got to his feet. "What time?"

"Six o'clock," I said.

Lestrade took his hat and coat from the rack near the door. "In that case, I will bid you gentlemen good night, and unless someone else gets themselves stabbed in the kidneys in the meantime, I will meet you tomorrow evening outside the Diogenes Club."

Lestrade took his leave, leaving Holmes and I to a quiet evening. I picked up my journal to record the events of the day, and Holmes reached for his violin. Soon the sounds of Bach flowed gently around our living room creating a soothing atmosphere in which to write.

Chapter Twelve

We arrived outside the Diogenes Club a few minutes before six o'clock to find Lestrade waiting for us.

"You could have gone inside, Lestrade," Holmes observed, as we approached him.

Lestrade shook his head. "Frankly, I would rather not have to deal with your brother any more than I have to. The level of power he has at his disposal is truly frightening."

We went through the doors into the elegant polished brass and marble foyer of the club. A liveried usher escorted us to the Stranger's Room, where Mycroft was waiting for us.

Mycroft Holmes was a man of imposing mental stature and almost horrific physique. His sedentary life circling between his rooms, his office in Whitehall, and his club, left him resembling a latter-day Falstaff, though his intellect far exceeded that of Shakespeare's knightly buffoon.

Comfortable chairs were set out for us, and Mycroft waved us to them as we came in, and proceeded to pour a little brandy for us all. "It is good to see you again, Sherlock," he said, as he handed his brother a glass. "And you too, Doctor Watson, Inspector Lestrade." We took the glasses offered to us as we took our seats.

"You are having an interesting time in Whitechapel?" Mycroft observed.

"As are you, it appears," Holmes replied. "If the charming Miss Watts' appearance at the soup kitchen is anything to go by."

"Indeed," Mycroft replied drily. "It is murder that takes you east?"

"You know it is," Holmes replied.

Mycroft tilted his head in acknowledgment. "The murder of John Geraghty; erroneously written off by a bigoted police officer as the result of a drunken brawl, and that of Jack Tyler, the Duncran Wharf representative of the newly formed Dock, Wharf, Riverside and General Labourers Union. A title that I doubt few of its members can even spell." He paused and took a sip of his brandy. "What links these murders to the soup kitchen?"

It was Lestrade who answered. "Probably nothing. The last person to see Jack Tyler alive was at the soup kitchen. Or outside of it."

"I see." Mycroft looked thoughtful. "And the fact both men were connected to Duncran Wharf?"

Holmes twitched irritably. "Enough, Mycroft! What do you know on the subject?"

"On the subject of the murders; no more than you, I suspect. But Duncran Wharf on the other hand…"

A thought darted across my mind and I leaned forward to ask eagerly, "Has your interest something to do with John Geraghty's suspicions of smuggling at Duncran Wharf?"

Mycroft gave me a startled look and then looked at his brother. "I congratulate you, Sherlock; the good doctor's observational skills are increasing." Not waiting for his brother to reply, Mycroft continued, "There are two matters that are under investigation by my agents for Her Majesty's government. The first one is possible foreign involvement in the dock strike."

"Foreign involvement?" Lestrade asked.

"Her Majesty's government suspects that the Germans are involved. The Kaiser, as you are no doubt aware, has little love for this country."

That was something of an understatement. Kaiser Wilhelm II loathed us. When his father, Kaiser Frederick III, lay dying the previous year, Wilhelm was heard to yell, "An English doctor crippled my arm and an English doctor is killing my father." Our monarch's German grandson was not the most stable of men. I know little of politics, but even I could foresee that we would have trouble with Germany somewhere down the road.

Holmes leaned forward, his expression intent. "What evidence do you have for German involvement? You must have something, Mycroft; you, of all people, do not go chasing shadows."

"We do not have much to go on," Mycroft admitted. "Just that the strike has been organized with the precision that the Germans are renowned for, and the fact that German guns are turning up in the hands of some of London's less upright citizens. Which is the second matter Miss Watts is investigating."

"Guns?" Holmes asked.

Mycroft nodded. "German small arms. M1879 Reichsrevolvers, to be precise."

Holmes frowned. "A six-shot revolver with a seven inch barrel, from memory. Not the easiest weapon to conceal, but not too obvious either. It would fit snuggly into the pocket of an overcoat, for example, but be a little harder to conceal elsewhere on the person."

Lestrade nodded. "I have seen a few over the years. They are German army service issue. Not too heavy to carry. They weigh about 2 and a half pounds. Not a weapon for a woman, but the average man could handle one easily enough." He frowned, "I trust Dorothy is armed? I would not like to think of her going up against a German agent unarmed."

Mycroft just looked at Lestrade. "Of course. Miss Watts has been trained with, and now carries in her reticule at all times, a Remington derringer. She has proven to be an extremely good shot. I have every confidence that if the situation arose that she would not hesitate to shoot to kill."

Holmes, I could tell, was not listening to this conversation.

Mycroft continued, "Miss Watts is ostensibly working at the soup kitchen as any young woman of independent means and high-mindedness might do. In reality she is attempting to track down the source of the guns as well as find evidence of German involvement in the strike."

"John Geraghty," Holmes said slowly, "...believed that there was smuggling going on at Duncran Wharf. He had been going through the papers attempting to find what was being smuggled and from where."

"What did he find?" Mycroft asked.

Holmes shook his head. "That I do not know, because after his death someone ransacked the papers in his office. The papers I was given had pages missing."

"It would be safe to assume that the missing pages relate to goods coming in from Germany," Lestrade observed.

"It is possible. In fact is it highly likely; however, we do not know that for certain, and must keep an open mind on the subject," Holmes replied.

"I agree," said Mycroft. "Sherlock, I only ask that you keep me informed of anything you may find, and that you do not compromise Miss Watts in any way."

Holmes got to his feet. "You may trust us all to be discreet, Mycroft. I think, though, that we need to talk to the Geraghty family again." He held up a hand when Mycroft seemed about to object. "We can ask about goods coming in from Germany and if they have seen any Germans around the wharf. Guns do not need to be mentioned. Nor any hypothetical involvement in the strike."

Mycroft frowned and then nodded. "It would be logical for you to take such a discovery to the owner of the wharf," he agreed. "Very well, Sherlock, gentlemen, I wish you a good evening and good hunting."

We took our leave of Mycroft and walked out into the balmy summer evening.

As we stood in the street, looking around for cabs, Lestrade asked "Do we go to the Geraghty's tonight?"

Holmes shook his head. "It is not so vital that we need to do that. Tomorrow morning will be fine. Besides, Whitechapel as darkness is falling is not a pleasant place to visit, no matter how genial the hosts."

"Tomorrow morning then," said Lestrade. "Shall I meet you there?"

"Come to Baker Street around nine o'clock. We shall go together."

Lestrade flagged down a cab. "Right you are. See you tomorrow then." He paused as he mounted the cab step. "Do you wish to share?"

Holmes shook his head. "It is a pleasant evening, Watson and I shall walk home." He looked at me. "If that is acceptable to you."

"It is fine Holmes. A little exercise will do us both good," I replied.

Lestrade laughed as he shut the cab door. He grinned at us out the window. "I gave up walking the beat when I became a detective. I see no good reason to take it up again."

We watched the cab drive away before commencing our walk back to Baker Street as around us London's night life came awake.

Chapter Thirteen

We had risen and breakfasted and were already waiting outside when the cab carrying Lestrade arrived. Rather than let him exit, we joined Lestrade inside and instructed the cabbie to take us to the address on Whitechapel High Street.

The roads were crowded with delivery vehicles and cabs, though, thankfully, very few private carriages at that time of the morning. Pedestrian traffic was also chaotic. People swirling between the vehicles; dashing from one side of the road to the other, or doggedly plodding along pushing handcarts laden with goods for sale.

It was a typical London morning. An altercation between another cabbie and a brewery dray driver held us up in Clerkenwell Road, but we made reasonably good time getting to Whitechapel.

Upon our arrival we were shown into the comfortable front parlour that we had been in previously. Michael Geraghty, his mother, and sister Julia promptly joined us.

"You have news for us?" Michael Geraghty asked eagerly.

Holmes shook his head. "Not yet. You are aware of the murder of Jack Tyler?"

"Yes. William told me. He was killed in the same manner as my brother, was he not?"

"He was," Lestrade said, "and quite possibly by the same man who killed your brother."

"That has yet to be proved," said Holmes. "For the moment it is sufficient to say that the two men, both of whom worked on Duncran Wharf, where killed in the same fashion."

"They almost have to be linked," Lestrade objected.

"But we do not know for sure that they are," said Holmes. "If we insist on saying that they are, without further evidence, then we run the risk of focusing purely upon facts that support that proposition and ignoring any that do not. That is not a wise course of action for a detective, be he of the consulting or Scotland Yard variety."

Lestrade took the mild rebuke with good grace and was silent.

Holmes turned back to the Geraghtys. "We have had some information come to us that may be linked to both murders."

"And that is?" Mrs. Geraghty asked curiously.

"Has anyone reported seeing a German hanging around the area? Not a dock worker, or resident, but one who is unfamiliar."

Michael shook his head, but, to my surprise, Julia spoke up. "William says that a strange man has been hanging around the picket line at the wharf."

"Do you know if this man is German, by any chance?" asked Holmes.

Julia nodded. "Yes. William has spoken to him. The man appeared to be annoying Peter. Peter is William's brother," Julia explained. "William thought he was just someone hanging around hoping to see some sort of violence on the picket line." She looked at us. "That has happened on the lines at some of the other wharves and docks."

Lestrade nodded his agreement. "My colleague at Leman Street, Inspector Reid, has spoken on the subject at some length."

"The man had quite a strong German accent. According the William the man told him that his name was Otto Bauer, and he was the clerk for a wine merchant on Fleet Street who was concerned about an incoming shipment of German wine," said Julia.

"He had the wrong wharf then," Michael commented. "We do not bring in wine. Wine and tobacco go through London Docks where there are customs men permanently stationed."

"What do you bring in, Mr. Geraghty?" asked Holmes.

"Haberdashery mostly. Good quality lace from Brussels, cotton fabric from Germany, and fine woven silk cloth from France. Occasionally Irish linen."

"And what do you send out?"

"Wool yarn and cloth, mostly. Though the heyday of British wool production has gone, the quality of what is still produced is far superior to most of that produced in Europe."

"Interesting," my friend commented. "Thank you for your time and for your assistance. You have been most helpful."

"Anything that will assist you to find the true killer of my brother, Mr. Holmes," Michael Geraghty replied, "I will be only too happy to do."

As we went to take our leave of the Geraghtys, Holmes commented. "We made the acquaintance of Mr. James Harrison the other day."

"Harrison?" Whatever for?" Michael Geraghty asked.

"I understand that he is endeavouring to purchase Duncran Wharf on behalf of the London and St. Katherine's Docks Company."

Michael Geraghty scowled. "He is." The scowl deepened. "You don't think that the company is behind the death of my brother and that of Jack Tyler, do you?"

Holmes shook his head. "It is possible, but I consider it unlikely. Harrison was involved with Tyler, of that much I am certain, but I do not think Harrison is capable of such cold-blooded murder. And I am equally certain that your brother would not have turned his back upon the man."

Michael Geraghty nodded thoughtfully. "That is true. John said once that he wouldn't trust Harrison even if the man had a letter signed by God attesting to his trustworthiness."

"It seems that your brother was an excellent judge of character," Holmes commented.

We left the Geraghty family and walked out onto the swirl of humanity that was Whitechapel. Even though it was summer, the miasma of smoke from the industries meant that such sunlight as filtered through was weak. I coughed to clear my throat and noted Lestrade was doing the same.

"Well, Holmes, what is our next move?" Lestrade asked.

"Out next move is a visit to Mycroft's office in Whitehall."

I blinked in some surprise. "What have you discovered that is so urgent that we must go to Mycroft's office now rather than at the Diogenes Club this evening?"

"Mycroft will want to know that the German government is most definitely involved somewhere in this case."

"The mysterious Otto Bauer?" asked Lestrade.

Holmes nodded. "I should like to know what Mycroft knows about him."

"If he knows anything," I said. "Surely the clerk for a wine merchant is beneath your brother's attention?"

"Have you not realized yet, Watson, that nothing and no-one is beneath Mycroft's attention? Especially if the object or the person pertains to the safety and security of this realm."

"You think he is a German spy?" asked Lestrade.

"I think it is a distinct possibility," said Holmes. "I also suspect that Duncran Wharf is the source of the guns now in London."

"How do you know?" I asked.

"The missing papers, Watson."

"What about them?"

"The papers William Blehane gave to me were incomplete, as you both know. I now know exactly what papers are missing."

"What?" I exclaimed. "But how?"

"A process of elimination, my friend. None of the papers delivered to me so much as mentioned Germany as a source of imported goods. Someone went to a great deal of trouble to ensure all mentions of Germany were removed."

"Not a very smart move, though," commented Lestrade. "Surely they must have realized that a few questions to anyone who works the wharf would uncover the link the Germany."

I frowned. "I think the killer panicked. He killed John Geraghty and then realized that killing him was not going to be enough. Perhaps he thought Geraghty had more actual evidence than suspicion. So he removed the papers."

"Well done, Watson!" Holmes cried.

Lestrade frowned. "Which means the killer is tied into Duncran Wharf somehow. A stranger would not know where John Geraghty's office was, nor where the papers were kept."

"So Tyler was killed because he knew who the murderer is?" I asked.

Holmes shook his head. "Not necessarily. We do not know what the motive was for killing Tyler. The murderer will have his reasons."

"If nothing else," Lestrade commented, "…the strike has made it impossible for any more guns to be smuggled in."

"And there, Lestrade, is the perfect motive for Tyler's murder. It may not be the exact motive, but Tyler was very vocal about keeping the strike going," said Holmes. "And whilst that suits Harrison because it pushes Duncran Wharf towards bankruptcy; an idle wharf will not suit our smugglers."

We had been walking along Whitechapel High Street as we talked. Holmes managed to flag down a cab. As it drew to a halt beside us, he looked at Lestrade and me. "Come, gentlemen, it is time we were off."

As we settled in the cab Holmes called out to the cabbie "Whitehall if you please, my good man."

With a chuck of the reins, the cabbie eased the cab into the flow of traffic and we headed back towards the more salubrious parts of London.

Chapter Fourteen

We were shown straight into Mycroft's office when we arrived. Mycroft's people, and Mycroft himself, knew that his brother was not here for idle reasons.

Mycroft's clerk fetched extra chairs and Mycroft waited until he had left the room to speak.

"You have found something." It was clearly a statement, not a question.

"We have," Holmes replied. "A German national has been seen around the picket line at Duncran Wharf."

"Do you know who he is?" Mycroft asked.

"According to Miss Julia Geraghty, the man gave his name as Otto Bauer," said Lestrade.

"Ah!" Mycroft sank back in his seat.

"You know the name, I take it?" said Holmes.

"Herr. Otto Bauer is a name not unknown to me," Mycroft acknowledged.

"He claims to be the clerk for a wine merchant," I said.

Mycroft nodded. "He is, or, rather, it is not all that he is."

"What else is he?" Lestrade asked.

"Herr. Bauer does indeed work as a clerk for a wine merchant in Fleet Street," Mycroft said. "And by all accounts is good at his job. It is the other places that he frequents, apart from his place of employment, that makes him of interest to Her Majesty's government."

"And those places are?" asked Holmes.

"He spends an inordinate amount of time in St. James Park feeding the ducks. That is, when he is not casually visiting one of the buildings in Carlton House Terrace."

"Which building would that be?" asked Lestrade.

Holmes looked at his brother. "9 Carlton House Terrace, perhaps?"

"As you say, Sherlock," Mycroft agreed.

"What is at 9 Carlton House Terrace?" I asked.

It was Lestrade who answered me. "The German Embassy. I should have realized when Mr. Holmes mentioned St. James Park."

I thought for a moment. "So apart from a hobby of feeding the ducks…"

Holmes shook his head. "Not a hobby, Watson, but subterfuge. If people are used to seeing him arrive with a few crusts of bread for the ducks, they will not notice him when he leaves the park and goes into the embassy. A ploy to make him seem as much a part of the area as the ducks."

Mycroft nodded. "And it would normally work, except for the fact that I have people watching both the park and the embassy every single day. Nothing goes in or out that I am not made aware of."

"The question is exactly how Otto Bauer is involved in this. Is he a murderer?"

Mycroft shook his head. "No. At least, not of John Geraghty or Jack Tyler. I have had Herr. Bauer under observation since before the murders occurred. Apart from his visits to the docks, the man does not frequent the East End. He lives in lodgings in Whitefriars Street, not far from where he works in Fleet Street."

I shook my head. "I am confused," I admitted. "I cannot see how smuggling guns into London could possibly destabilize the government."

"That depends, my dear Watson," said Holmes "...on who is receiving the guns."

Mycroft took pity on my confusion. "Have you heard of Clan na Gael?"

I shook my head.

"I have," said Lestrade. "They are an offshoot of the Irish Republican Brotherhood. Clan na Gael was responsible for the bombing campaign a few years ago. They even bombed Scotland Yard."

I frowned, as I searched my memory. "Was that the bomb that destroyed the Special Irish Branch office?"

"It was," said Mycroft. "The bomb was placed in a public urinal." His tone conveyed his deep distaste at the very idea.

"What has this to do with guns?" I asked. I could understand dynamite being smuggled into London, but why guns?

"Clan na Gael is based in America, as I am sure you know," Mycroft said. "One of our people sent word that some high ranking members of Clan na Gael have been seen with known German agents. It was shortly after we learned this, that German small arms began turning up in the hands of London's criminal element. Monro was concerned and he came to me."

James Monro, currently Commissioner of the London Metropolitan Police, was both wary of Mycroft Holmes and aware that the man had enormous power and reach. It was clear that after becoming embroiled in the murderous affair that had ended on Westminster Bridge, Monro and Mycroft had come to some sort of mutually beneficial arrangement.

Lestrade frowned. "It makes no sense."

"Oh?" Holmes looked at Lestrade; eyebrows raised quizzically.

"Guns into the hands of Fenians, I can understand," said Lestrade. "These people will stop at nothing to gain freedom for Ireland, as the bombing campaign has shown. But putting guns in the hands of ordinary crooks makes no sense. Yes, they will use them in illegal pursuits, but it will not spread terror the way the bombings did."

Holmes shook his head. "My dear Lestrade, you are assuming that criminals getting access to guns is the point of the exercise."

"And you don't?"

Holmes shook his head. "I do not. I suspect that the situation is a lot more confused than we think."

"I am confused enough, thank you," I muttered under my breath.

Holmes ignored me. "Let us assume that the guns are being smuggled into London from the German government to Clan na Gael."

I nodded.

"We know that some guns, at least, are ending up with known criminals rather than unknown Fenians. What does that suggest to you?" Holmes asked.

Lestrade swore softly as the penny dropped. "Someone is stealing from Clan na Gael."

"Precisely," said Holmes. "Somewhere between the guns arriving at Duncran Wharf and the Fenians taking delivery of them, some of them are disappearing. Someone is in business for themselves."

"The Clan na Gael will not take kindly to that," Mycroft observed.

I frowned. "Is it possible that they are aware of what is happening and that is why there have been murders?"

Holmes shook his head. "That predisposes that both John Geraghty and Jack Tyler were members of Clan na Gael. I would like to have some evidence of that before we go starting that particular hare. It is a good thought, though, Watson."

I nodded. "What do we do now?"

Holmes looked at Mycroft. "I would like to have a word with Otto Bauer."

Mycroft sighed. "I was hoping you would not want that. We really do not want the Germans knowing how closely they are being watched."

Holmes sniffed. "If the Germans do not have a watch set on your office they are not nearly as organized as you believe them to be."

Lestrade spoke up. "Herr. Bauer was seen near Duncran Wharf and two men who worked there have been murdered. It is only natural that the police would wish to speak with anyone who was frequenting the area at the time."

"Very well," said Mycroft, after a thoughtful pause. "At this time of day he will be at his place of employment."

Mycroft told us the address on Fleet Street.

We left Mycroft's office shortly after that, and hailed a cab to take us to the wine merchants where Otto Bauer worked.

Rutherford and Sons: Wine Merchants of Quality occupied a charming 17th century shop front close by St. Bride's Church.

A cheerful, white-haired older man, with the ruddy complexion that one associates with the imbibing of good wines, greeted us as we entered the premises.

"A good day to you, gentlemen. Welcome to Rutherford and Sons. I am Josiah Rutherford. How can I help you today?"

Holmes nudged Lestrade forward. The inspector took the hint. "A good day to you, Mr. Rutherford. I am Inspector Lestrade of Scotland Yard, and this is Mr. Sherlock Holmes and Doctor John Watson. We would like to have a word with one of your employees, if he is about."

"And the employee would be?" Mr. Rutherford asked.

"Otto Bauer," Lestrade replied.

Rutherford frowned. "Is Otto in trouble?"

Holmes stepped in quickly. "On the contrary, my good sir. We understand that Bauer spends time around the docks?"

Rutherford nodded. "He does. Some of it for me, checking on incoming shipments, and some of it for himself."

Lestrade raised his eyebrows in query. Rutherford went on to explain, "Otto was born close to the Rhine. He likes to be near the river; he tells me. He says it reminds him of home."

Lestrade nodded. "There have been several murders close to the docks…"

Rutherford snorted. "There are always murders close to the docks. I swear a day does not go by that someone isn't murdered down there. It is why Otto insists on going there on my behalf. He says he is afraid someone will kill me because with my age and look of prosperity I look like an easy target."

"Interesting," Holmes commented. "But why do your sons not go?"

Rutherford looked at him blankly.

"The business is Rutherford and *Sons* after all."

Rutherford gave a short bark of laughter. "You are looking at the 'sons' part of the business, Mr. Holmes. The business was started by my great-grandfather. He had sons, as did my grandfather. I had a brother, but he died young of cholera.

I have never had the opportunity to marry. The business ends with me."

"I can understand why Bauer is so solicitous of your health," I commented.

"Indeed," Rutherford said. "Without me, poor Otto has no employment. Though I will probably leave him the business in my will. He is a good worker, and the customers like him. He is down in the cellar at the moment. I will fetch him for you."

With that, Rutherford walked into the back of the shop. We heard footsteps descending, then muffled voices, and two sets of footsteps ascending.

Rutherford came back into the shop, accompanied by a tall, thin, young man, with watchful blue eyes and a shuttered expression. His voice, when he spoke, held only the faintest hint of a German accent, not the heavy accent that Miss Geraghty had mentioned. "Mr. Rutherford tells me that you wish to speak to me about some murders." His tone held quiet bewilderment.

"If we may, Mr. Bauer." I noted that Lestrade used the English rather than German honorific.

Bauer shrugged as he came out from behind the counter. "I do not know what help I can give you gentlemen, but I will certainly try. But perhaps, not here? The customers, you understand."

"Of course," Lestrade replied. He gestured to the door. "Shall we?"

Holmes and I proceeded Bauer out of the door, with Lestrade bringing up the rear.

Once out on the street, Bauer turned to us. "I do not understand how you think I can help you. I am simply a clerk. I know nothing about murder."

"Never said you did, Mr. Bauer," said Lestrade. "But you do spend a lot of time by the docks."

Bauer raised his eyebrows. "Is this a crime in London? To spend time beside the river?"

"Not a crime," Lestrade said, "But there are certainly more pleasant places along the Thames than around the docks. Chelsea, for example."

Bauer shrugged. "I grew up in an area not unlike the docks. It reminds me of home."

"You have been spending time around Duncran Wharf," Holmes observed.

Bauer frowned. "Is that the little wharf with the loud mouthed man outside of it?"

Lestrade's moustache twitched with irritation. Bauer could not possibly as ingenuous as he seemed. I had to admit that the German was starting to annoy me as well.

"You know which wharf it is, Mr. Bauer," Lestrade said firmly, "You have been hanging around outside it watching the strikers often enough."

Bauer shrugged. "What do you want from me, Inspector? I visit the area. I mind my own business. I have seen no murder, nor yet done any." He looked at us, and for a moment the mild-mannered clerk disappeared and was replaced with a cold-eyed, harsh-mannered individual. "I cannot assist you, gentlemen, therefore I wish you a good day." He turned his back on us and walked back into the shop. The door banging closed behind him with a note of finality.

Lestrade reached for the door handle. Holmes placed his hand upon his wrist. "Leave it, Lestrade. Now is not the time."

"Damn it, Holmes! He knows something!" Lestrade exploded.

"I tend to agree," Holmes said. "But we will not get anything out of him. Not here and not now."

"I have a good mind to clap the darbies on him and drag him to the Yard," Lestrade grumbled.

"I doubt Mycroft would be too pleased with that," Holmes observed. "Come, Bauer knows that we know something. I shall set my Irregulars to watching both the shop and the man. We shall soon learn his secrets."

"You think your street arabs are better than your brother's spies?" Lestrade asked.

"I do not think so," Holmes said, as he turned to walk along the street. "I know so. My lads can get into places that Mycroft's agents can only dream of." With that, he walked away, leaving Lestrade and I to follow behind.

Chapter Fifteen

Lestrade returned to Scotland Yard, and Holmes and I went back to Baker Street, where Holmes sent for Wiggins.

The lad came promptly, lounging in the doorway of our rooms. "I 'ear you 'as a job for us, Mr. 'Olmes?"

"I do, Wiggins, lad. You know Rutherford and Sons?"

"The bloke what flogs wine on Fleet Street? Yeah. We knows 'im."

"He has a clerk…"

"The stuffy Kraut?" Wiggins grinned. "'E's a rum cove that one."

"In what way?" I asked. Wiggins was an observant boy who had risen to the position of leader of Holmes' Irregulars by dint of his intelligence and organizational abilities.

"When 'e ain't working, 'e's down the Chapel or the docks. Not with the wagtails or dollymops, mind, but chatting to the strikers. 'Oo goes down there to talk? No-one, that's 'oo."

"Interesting," Holmes observed. He handed Wiggins some coins, which the lad put carefully into his pocket. "Watch him, Wiggins. I want to know everywhere he goes and everyone he talks to."

"Will do, guv." Wiggins touched his right forefinger to his greasy cap and slipped out of the room and down the stairs.

Holmes turned to me. "And now, Watson comes the hardest part of any case."

"Waiting?" I asked.

"Waiting," Holmes agreed.

We did not have long to wait. The very next day a uniformed constable from Scotland Yard appeared in our doorway.

"Begging your pardon, Mr. Holmes, but Inspector Lestrade requests that you and Doctor Watson join him and Inspector Reid in Wapping," the young man said, his face creased in a frown of concentration. He had obviously learned the message by rote. His sharp features made him look like an extremely large, blue, parrot.

"What on earth is in Wapping?" I asked.

Holmes turned from where he was reaching for his coat, "Another corpse, I presume."

"Another corpse?"

"Why else would we be sent for, if not for the murder of Robert Glasheen?"

I stopped dead in the act of reaching for my coat. The young constable was giving Holmes a look a pure suspicion.

"Robert Glasheen?"

"Oh! Come now, Watson. Surely you remember that Glasheen lives in Wapping? Above his father's shop, I believe Inspector Reid said."

He glanced at the constable who was now staring openmouthed at him. "That is where we are going, is it not, constable?"

The constable shook himself. "Yes, Mr. Holmes. To a general merchandise shop in Wapping. I've a cab out front waiting to take us there."

"Excellent." He turned to me, "Come, Watson! Do not let us keep the good inspectors waiting." He shrugged into his coat and walked out the door.

I put my own coat on, and went to follow. The constable touched my arm and whispered, "Is he always like that, Doctor Watson?"

I looked down the stairs at the back of my departing friend. I could not forebear a small smile. "No, lad."

The constable relaxed slightly.

"Sometimes he is much worse."

I followed Holmes down the stairs leaving the confused constable to bring up the rear.

Chapter Sixteen

Holmes was silent in the cab to Wapping. I gazed out the window at the hustle and bustle of London's East End.

Wapping is a very old part of London. There have been docks at Wapping since at least the sixteenth century, probably much earlier. Wapping was the site of the infamous Execution Dock where river pirates were hanged, including the notorious Captain Kidd. It was also the place where the River Police, London's first police force, regardless of what their counterparts at Scotland Yard said, was formed.

Close by was the Ratcliffe Highway where the notorious Ratcliffe Highway Murders, with the bizarre disposal of the body of the alleged murderer, had taken place in 1811. All in all, Wapping was a dark, dank, and extremely depressing part of London.

The cab drew up outside a shop on the Wapping High Street. The street was close to the river and the smell of water-borne garbage and the screech of the sea gulls did little to add to the ambience of the area. Our cab driver was obviously of the same mind, because as soon as we had exited the cab, he was briskly trotting away, intent on getting out of Wapping as soon as he could.

The shop that we had alighted in front of had clearly seen better times. The brickwork was grubby and the painted wooden sign above the door was peeling. The sign was still legible though; faded though the letters were. It read "Glasheen's

General Goods and Groceries." Barrels and assorted boxes were visible through the grimy windows. Now two uniformed constables stood sentry outside its closed doors.

"A depressing place," Holmes commented.

"More than most," Lestrade said, coming out of the shop. "Especially for Patrick and Ellen Glasheen, proprietors of this business. Business is down with the dock strike, and now their eldest son has been murdered in his room."

"In his room, you say?" Holmes turned to Lestrade, eyebrows raised in query.

Lestrade nodded. "Similar situation to Jack Tyler." He grimaced, "Though the room is much cleaner than the one Tyler was living in."

We followed Lestrade into the shop. A long, L-shaped, wooden counter dominated two sides of the room. The counter and the shelves behind it were stacked with groceries. Two large barrels, one marked "sugar" and the other "flour" sat side by side beneath the window.

Directly behind the counter and in line with the door to the street, a curtained doorway led into the recesses of the premises. From behind there I could hear the sounds of a woman weeping in some considerable distress.

"Robert Glasheen's mother, Ellen," Lestrade said softly, noting my look. "She found his body when she went to call him down to breakfast."

Holmes was looking around, a slight frown on his face. "How did the killer gain entry?"

Inspector Reid, coming through the curtained doorway, replied, "There is an entrance into the building from the back alley. From there it is straight up the stairs to Robert Glasheen's room."

"And the parents?" Holmes asked. "Where do they sleep that they were not disturbed by the killer?"

Reid thumbed back over his shoulder. "In a room just through there. They've had problems with thieves over the years, so they prefer to sleep close to the main shop front. Also the stairs have got a little hard for Mrs. Glasheen. She spent years as a washerwoman and now suffers from rheumatism in her knees."

"Yet she went upstairs to wake her son," Holmes observed.

"He was late to breakfast and did not respond to her calls. Patrick had already opened the shop, so Ellen dragged herself up there." Reid shook his head. "Her screams brought Patrick and a customer up. The customer took one look and ran for a constable."

Reid raised a flap in the counter and gestured to us to come through. "I'll take you up."

We followed Reid through the curtain into a comfortable room that belied the worn and rundown image of the building.

A woman of late middle-age was seated on a well-padded sofa being comforted by a much younger woman. An older man stood behind the sofa wringing his hands is if he did not quite know what to do with them.

The younger woman's resemblance to Robert Glasheen made it clear that she was some relation, quite possibly a sister. She looked up at Reid.

"As soon as Tommy brought me the news, I came over, Edmund. I could not leave mother alone for this."

"Of course not, Mary. That's why I sent Tommy to tell you," Reid replied.

The woman, Mary, flashed Reid a tight little smile before drawing her mother closer to her and making gentle soothing noises.

Reid led the way through the room and out into a well-appointed kitchen. The only sign that anything untoward had happened was the meal left untouched and abandoned upon the table.

Reid turned to us. "That was Robert's sister, Mary, in case you were wondering. She is married to a policeman. Tommy Jenkins. A good lad. He'll make sergeant soon."

A narrow stairway to the right led upstairs, and Reid headed up there trusting us to follow.

At the top of the stairs an equally narrow hallway led along the floor. Three doors remained closed, but a fourth stood open and had another two uniformed constables standing guard.

The sight that met our eyes, as we stood in the doorway, was not a pleasant one. Robert Glasheen lay slumped face down across a bed. He was still clad in his day time clothes. Blood had dried across the back of his clean, but well-worn, shirt, indicating that he, like John Geraghty and Jack Tyler, had been stabbed in the kidneys. It was no wonder that his poor mother had screamed upon seeing her son. It was obvious even to a layman that Robert Glasheen was dead and had been for quite some time.

More noise from downstairs heralded the arrival of H Division's police surgeon, George Bagster Phillips. He greeted Reid cheerfully and nodded to us. Eyeing the corpse laying across the bed he said, "Nominally, Edmund, I will say that the deceased died in the same manner as Jack Tyler. As to anything else, you will have to wait until I perform the post-mortem examination."

"I wouldn't expect anything else from you, George," Reid replied.

Phillips smiled briefly and turned to signal to a couple of brawny fellows who were lurking in the hallway. They came in, carrying a large length of canvas and several ropes. They swiftly wrapped the corpse of Robert Glasheen, bound the body tight with the ropes, and maneuvered their grisly burden out of the room and down the stairs to where a large covered barrow no doubt waited in the street.

An outburst of loud wailing signaled that the corpse was being taken through the parlour and out through the shop.

Inspector Reid winced. "Good God, man! Why wasn't the body taken out the back? His poor mother…"

Doctor Phillips shrugged. "Nothing I could do about it, Edmund. The laneway at the rear is too small to get the barrow down. We tried. I will leave some laudanum for the poor lady when I go."

"Be prepared to get an earful from Mary," Reid warned. "She is not going to be happy."

Phillips sighed. "I do not blame her." He touched his hat to us in farewell and left the room. A few moments later we heard the sound of a female voice raised in anger, followed by Doctor Phillips' deeper voice gently placating.

Holmes continued to study the room from his place in the doorway.

The room was a lot more homely than that of poor Jack Tyler. It was scrupulously clean; the well-worn floorboards scrubbed and polished. I suspected by the hand of a maid, or the sister, Mary, rather than the rheumatic mother.

A single window in one wall looked out upon the narrow alley-way of which Doctor Phillips had complained. The bed sat beneath the window; the head board of the heavy iron bedstead carefully lined up in line with the window sill above.

A bed box sat at the foot of the bed, and a battered chest of drawers sat against the right hand wall. An old wooden chair sat beside it with a coat draped carelessly across it. A pair of trousers lay bunched up on the floor beneath the chair.

The room was devoid of both decoration and personality. It could have been a room in a better class lodging house rather than a room in what was, to all intents and purposes, a family home.

Holmes stepped into the room and began to gaze around, his expression intent.

Reid opened his mouth to speak, but Lestrade laid a hand upon his arm, shaking his head. Reid quirked an eyebrow at him, but shut his mouth.

Holmes turned back to Reid, "I trust that this time the corpse was examined before it was shifted?"

"Yes, Mr. Holmes," Reid replied with another slight wince. "I did so myself before you gentlemen arrived."

Holmes nodded and turned his attention to the bed, whisking the blankets off and inspecting the mattress carefully. "No hiding place made in there, but I suspect Glasheen would have been wary of using his bed as a hiding place."

"Why?" Reid asked.

"I very much doubt that he made his own bed of a morning, Inspector. Too much risk of someone else discovering whatever he chose to hide."

"Why do you think he was hiding something?" Lestrade asked.

Holmes shot him an irritated look. "Something got him killed, Lestrade. Men with nothing to hide rarely get murdered in such a fashion. Glasheen was hiding something; what that something was is what we need to discover."

I found myself staring at the coat on the chair. Holmes noticed my distraction.

"What is it, Watson?" he asked.

"You may think I am a fool…"

"Never that, my friend," Holmes assured me.

"But there is something wrong with the way that coat is hanging, but for the life of me I cannot put my finger on what is wrong."

Lestrade bent down and retrieved the garment from off the chair. "You're right, Doctor Watson," he said, with a frown, there is something heavy in the pocket that is making it hang all wrong."

He went to put his hand in the pocket.

"Careful, Giles," Reid said. "I've known men to put mouse traps in the pockets to prevent pick-pockets getting their money."

Lestrade paused, then took the coat over to the bed and shook it vigorously. A large metal object fell from the coat pocket and into the middle of the bed.

It was a revolver.

We stood staring at it.

"A gun?" said Reid with a note of disbelief in his voice.

"A M1879 Reichsrevolver to be precise," Holmes said.

I understood now why the coat was hanging wrong and why I had not recognized it for what it was. The M1879 was a different shape and size from my old service revolver.

"Why would Robert Glasheen have a gun?" Reid asked. "And more importantly, where did he get it?" He caught Lestrade's look of slight amusement. "Yes, Giles, I know anything can be bought on the streets of London, but rarely guns. Not amongst his sort."

Holmes was turning the gun over in his hands. He looked up at Reid. "Let us just say that the government has been aware for a while that unauthorized weapons have been coming into the country via London's docks."

Reid stared at him for a moment then groaned. "Wonderful. Anarchists or Fenians?"

"Who is to say it is either?" Holmes asked.

"Don't give me any flannel, Mr. Holmes," Reid said crisply. "I have policed this city for years. Your average crook hasn't got the intelligence to work a gun. A knife in the dark is more their speed. Guns are almost always used by insurgents employing terror as a weapon. And in London that means Anarchists or Fenians."

"You are wasted as a police officer, Inspector Reid, you would have made an excellent consulting detective," Holmes said. "You are correct. The government suspects Fenians, or rather, one of their offshoots. The Clan na Gael."

Reid frowned. "I had not heard that Glasheen, or any of the other Duncran Wharf workers had allegiance to Clan na Gael. But that doesn't mean that they don't. I shall ask around."

"Be careful, Inspector Reid," Holmes advised. "It is suspected that the guns are coming in via Duncran Wharf."

"I think it is a little more than a suspicion now," said Lestrade, nodding at the gun that Holmes still held in his hands.

Holmes shook his head. "Not so, Lestrade. Glasheen had the gun but he may have got it from somewhere else. I agree that Duncran Wharf looks like the most likely place for the guns to be entering, but one gun in the possession of a single wharf labourer does not mean the wharf itself is the source of the weapon."

Lestrade thought about it for a moment and then sighed. "Just for once I would like a case that is open and shut."

Holmes ignored him, carefully wrapping the gun in a handkerchief and placing it in his coat pocket. When Reid objected, Holmes shook his head. "Certain people in the government need to see this. Trust me, Inspector, the less you know, the happier you will be."

"I won't be happy, Mr. Holmes, until the murderer is behind bars waiting to swing from a rope," Inspector Reid replied.

"A sentiment that we can all agree with," Holmes replied.

We left the room, heading downstairs and into the front room where Mary Jenkins was waiting for us. She led us into the kitchen out the back.

"I have put mother to bed with a little of Doctor Phillips's laudanum. However, I do not wish to leave her alone for long, so I will be brief."

"Anything you can tell us, Mary, will be helpful," Reid replied.

Mary sighed. "Robbie was a fool, and what is worse, he was a fool with romantic ideas."

"Romantic ideas?" asked Reid.

"Romantic is the politest word for them," the woman replied.

I wondered briefly if the young man had been involved in some sort of love triangle.

"Can you elaborate, Mary, please?" asked Reid.

"Robbie was in love with the idea of an Irish homeland. The idiot had become involved with Clan na Gael." She held up a hand. "And before you ask Edmund, I found out by accident, and could get no details from him as to whom the other members were."

Mary smiled a little bitterly. "He told me that he knew very little anyway because he wasn't completely trusted on account of me being married to an English policeman. As if Tommy wasn't a fine, good-natured man."

Inspector Reid nodded. "Tommy has a good future ahead of him."

"Robbie begged me not to tell our parents and I agreed, fool that I am. Maybe if I had said something, nothing would have happened."

Holmes shook his head. "I very much doubt that, Mrs. Jenkins. The men who make up the Clan na Gael care for little. If they thought their security had been compromised, it is just as likely they would have burned this place to the ground while everyone slept. Do not think harshly of yourself."

"Does Tommy know?" Reid asked.

Mary shook her head. "No. If I could not tell my parents, I dared not tell Tommy. It would have put him in an awful situation. I was trying to think of a way to let you know without dragging Tommy into it."

Reid nodded, and patted her shoulder comfortingly.

We took our leave of that sad household. Reid headed back to Leman Street. Holmes, Lestrade and I walked through Whitechapel until we could get a cab to take us back to Marylebone.

We were in desperate need of a fortifying cup of tea by the time we reached Baker Street.

When we went inside, Holmes popped his head into the kitchen to request tea and sandwiches; a request to which Mrs. Hudson readily agreed.

"It is a trifle early for food, is it not, Holmes?" I asked when we reached our rooms.

Holmes shrugged out of his coat and hung it up. He took the gun from out of his pocket and locked it inside his desk.

He turned to me, "I am expecting a visitor, Watson. He will be hungry. He always is."

"A visitor?" Lestrade asked, struggling out of his own coat. "Who are you expecting?"

"Wiggins," Holmes replied. "I spotted him as we came out of Glasheen's shop. He will no doubt be here shortly."

Mrs. Hudson came bustling in with a tea tray, which I took from her with a word of thanks, and placed it upon the table.

I poured us all a cup and offered around the plates of comestibles. Holmes took the tea but refused the food. Lestrade took both, as did I.

Lestrade took a sip of his tea before commenting, "Wiggins is a sharp lad. He and Archie did well with the Molly-Boy case."

"How is Archie?" I asked.

Archie, one of Holmes's brightest Irregulars had gone to live with one of the sergeants from A Division at the conclusion of the Molly-Boy case. The lad was getting an education and had enthusiastically declared his desire to become a policeman.

Lestrade chuckled. "Sergeant Halliday tells me he is doing well. The lad is learning his letters and his sums. He is also shooting up like a weed on Mrs. Halliday's cooking."

Holmes smiled. "That is good to hear."

A knocking on the door downstairs, followed by the sound of boots on the stairs, heralded the arrival of Wiggins.

"Mornin' Mr. 'Olmes," he said.

"A good morning to you too, Wiggins." Holmes waved at the table. "Have a cup of tea and some sandwiches and tell us what you have learned. You have learned something, have you not? Otherwise you would not have tried so hard to catch my eye in Wapping."

Wiggins grinned as he carefully filled a plate with roast beef and watercress sandwiches, and several of Mrs. Hudson's excellent scones with raspberry jam and cream. I poured the lad a cup of tea to which he liberally added milk and sugar, before sitting back in his seat and beginning to eat.

Holmes waited until the lad had taken the edge off his hunger before asking. "Well, Wiggins, what have you discovered?"

"I bin followin' the Kraut like you asked," Wiggins began.

Lestrade blinked. "Bauer?" he asked me.

"Bauer," I confirmed.

"The Kraut's bin spendin' a lot o' time at the docks like you said. Jus' walkin;' around chattin' to people. People a cove like 'im shouldn't rightly be talkin' to," said Wiggins.

"Such as?" Holmes asked.

Wiggins drained his tea cup and looked into it sadly. I rose from my seat and refilled the lad's cup. He beamed at me happily.

Wiggins returned his attention to Holmes. "'E's bin 'angin' around Duncran Wharf a lot. I fink 'e finds the strike interestin'. 'E's bin chatting to the strikers. They mostly don't give 'im the time o' day. But yesterdee I seed him talkin' with the cove 'oo got 'isself killed."

"Robert Glasheen?" Lestrade asked.

Wiggins nodded. "They was talkin' away from the wharf. Near the soup kitchen. Not right in front o' it, but in the alley out back. Like they didn't wanna be seen."

"That is very interesting," Holmes commented. "Well done, Wiggins lad." He reached into his pocket and dug out some coins which he handed to Wiggins. The boy tucked them away safely. "Ta, Mr. 'Olmes." He nodded to Lestrade and me, and hurried out of the flat.

Lestrade looked at Holmes. "Back to Fleet Street?"

"Back to Fleet Street," Holmes agreed.

Chapter Seventeen

A cab took us back to Rutherford and Sons: Wine Merchants. Otto Bauer was not pleased to see us when we walked in the door.

He turned as if to move into the back of the shop.

"A word, Mr. Bauer, if you please," said Lestrade. "Here or at Scotland Yard. The choice is yours."

Bauer glared at Lestrade. "You cannot take me to Scotland Yard. I have done nothing wrong. I am a respectable gentleman."

"I will be the judge on all three of those points," Lestrade said drily.

"Herr Bauer." Holmes's tone was cold. "You have again been seen in places unbecoming the gentleman you claim to be. And now a man with whom you were observed holding a conversation is dead."

Bauer shrugged. "Men die every day, Herr Holmes."

"That is true," Holmes said. "Although not usually with a knife driven into their kidneys."

Bauer looked startled for a moment, then schooled his face back into an expression of impassiveness. "If a man has been murdered, what has it to do with me? I speak to many men every day."

Lestrade raised his eyebrows. "You hang around the soup kitchen in Whitechapel everyday talking to striking dock labourers? Looking for a ruffer were you?" Lestrade was clearly choosing to both deliberately misunderstand Bauer's meaning and be as offensive as it was possible to be.

Bauer's eyes blazed. He may not have understand what Lestrade's slang meant, but he understood the tone and the implication. "I think you insult me, Inspector. I think you mean to goad me into saying something you can arrest me for. I repeat: I have done nothing wrong. I have no desire to talk to you. To any of you. Please leave this shop."

Lestrade grinned viciously and turned and walked out. Holmes and I followed him.

"What on earth was that about, Lestrade?" Holmes said.

"I know his sort, Holmes," Lestrade replied. "We could talk until we are blue in the face, and he will say nothing. But infer that he is less than a gentleman and you will rattle him. Once rattled, he will not be thinking too clearly, and is more likely to do something to lead us to the killer."

Holmes looked at him for a long moment, and then shook his head, obviously holding on to his temper with the greatest effort of will. "I think you are wrong, Lestrade. But what is done is done; the situation cannot be salvaged now."

"What shall we do now?" I asked.

Holmes thought for a moment. "I believe it is time that we called upon the Geraghty family again. To ask what they know of Clan na Gael working on their wharf. Come, Watson."

We walked away along Fleet Street in search of a cab, leaving Lestrade to hurry to catch up with us.

The Geraghty family were all at home when we arrived. We were seated once again in the parlour, by the maid. Mrs. Geraghty and Julia supplied a large pot of excellent Ceylon tea, and an array of sandwiches and slices of a particularly fine Victoria sponge cake.

For once it was not my friend who was impatient with the ritual of British teatime. After a couple of sips of his tea, Michael Geraghty put his cup down and turned to my friend.

"Mr. Holmes, do you have any idea what is going on? I learned today that I have lost another worker with the murder of Robert Glasheen. Is someone trying to destroy my business by killing off my workers one by one?"

Holmes shook his head. "An interesting idea, but I do not believe that to be the case, Mr. Geraghty. Duncran Wharf is the battlefield, but not the battle itself." He took a sip of his own tea. "Tell me, Mr. Geraghty, what do you know of Clan na Gael?"

Michael Geraghty leaned back in his seat, scowling ferociously. "So that's it, is it? I have thrice damned Fenians on my wharf."

"We have reason to believe," Holmes continued, "that Robert Glasheen may have been a member of Clan na Gael. Quite possibly Jack Tyler was as well. As for your brother…"

"John was no Fenian," Mrs. Geraghty said firmly. "None of my children are. My husband, my dearest departed Michael, did not hold with such nonsense. He and I raised our children to believe that anything that one has to murder for is not worth having. To kill another is to imperil your immortal soul. To kill for a few yards of dirt…"

"I am not saying you are incorrect, mother, Julia interrupted. "But some wrongs go deep. William's uncle and one of his cousins were murdered by the police in Galway when they went to visit a dying relative, and his father is in Strangeways. Imprisoned on the evidence of lying policemen."

She looked at us. "He took lace samples to Manchester to show a buyer. The police accused him of theft. Nothing that we could say or do would convince them otherwise. To them he was obviously a thieving Irishman."

None of us quite knew what to say to that.

"The Fenians espouse the beliefs of the Anarchists in some measure," Holmes said softly. "That terror is a legitimate weapon to be used against the government and the populace."

Lestrade pulled a sour face. "Five years ago the Fenians bombed Scotland Yard. It is not something I will forget in a hurry, and I am trained, in some measure, to deal with shocking brutality. The average person is not and cannot deal with such things that are beyond their experience."

"Hence the use of weapons against the people," Holmes said. "The government will not give in. To concede to the demands of the Fenians is perceived as weakness, and so the terror will continue." I could almost hear the echo of Mycroft's voice in my friend's words.

Mrs. Geraghty sighed and folded her hands in her lap. "'Tis a wicked world we live in, and no mistake."

"Indeed, ma'am," Holmes replied.

"As my mother said," Michael Geraghty spoke up, "John was no Fenian. Our attitude to them, bar my sister's fire on behalf of her swain," he smiled at Julia who merely sniffed and turned away. "...is well known, which is most likely why I had no knowledge that they were working on my wharf. Could John have found out about them, Mr. Holmes? Is that why he was murdered?"

"It is one of the things we are looking at, Mr. Geraghty," Holmes said.

We took our leave from the family shortly after that. As we stood in the street, Lestrade looked around and sighed. "One of the things were are looking at?"

"I have a few ideas," Holmes said softly. "Certainly more than I had before this morning."

"That is something, at least," Lestrade said.

It was left to me to ask, yet again, "What shall we do now?"

"Go home, my dear Watson. I need to think and the noise of the streets is not conducive to that," Holmes replied.

Lestrade returned to Scotland Yard and we returned to Marylebone.

Back in our rooms, Holmes settled down in his chair with a pipe of tobacco and a faraway look in his eyes. I knew better than to disturb him when he was in this mood.

I settled down to write up my case notes. By the time I had finished, Holmes was on his third pipe, and the room was getting decidedly fuggy. I debated opening a window, then decided a walk in the fresh air and calm greenness of Regent's Park would serve the same purpose and be less likely to provoke complaints from Holmes that I was interrupting his thought processes.

I returned some two hours later to find the windows open to clear the air and Holmes poring bright-eyed over a map of London's East End. I noted he had marked various points upon the map: Duncran Wharf, the Geraghtys' house, and the Ten Bells Public House among them.

"You have more than just ideas," I observed as I took off my hat and coat.

Holmes shook his head. "Ideas and suspicions, that is all. I have no evidence, Watson. I need evidence."

"You will get it," I said.

"Your confidence in me is touching, but possibly misplaced," Holmes replied as he carefully folded up his map. "Now, what about a spot of dinner at Simpson's?"

"Sounds like an excellent idea to me," I said as I put my coat and hat back on.

Chapter Eighteen

We had a pleasant dinner at Simpson's and walked back to our rooms through the enjoyable summer night.

Well-fed and content, I slept deeply and was only woken by Holmes shaking my shoulder the next morning.

"Come, Watson."

"What is it, Holmes?"

"There has been another murder."

I sat bolt upright in my bed and gazed at my friend, aghast. "Who is it?"

"Otto Bauer," Holmes replied. "A message has just come from Lestrade."

I hastened out of my bed and into my clothes.

I followed Holmes downstairs and into the cab that was waiting patiently at the curb. It was still early and the air was cool and relatively fresh. The traffic was reasonably light and we made good time as we headed into the City itself.

Whitefriars Street got its name from the Carmelite monastery of the White Friars that had been established in the area in the 13th century. Much later the area had been known as the notorious Alsatia, a strange sanctuary for all manner of villains and ne'er-do-wells.

These days Whitefriars Street held a renowned glass works, lodging houses and a few newspapers that could not find tenancy on the slightly more prestigious Fleet Street.

It was easy enough to find Bauer's lodgings. An extremely disgruntled Lestrade was standing in the street outside it. He spoke not a word but led us down a small alley-way to the rear of the building. Several uniformed constables stood near a rear fence about a yard from the rear of the building.

Crumpled against a door at the top of some steps leading into the building was the corpse of Otto Bauer, incongruously clad in a nightshirt and slippers. A scattering of small pebbles lay beside the steps.

Holmes looked at the body for a long moment without speaking, before turning to Lestrade and saying "You said Bauer would lead us to the killer. It looks more as if we led the killer to him."

"What do you mean, Holmes?" I asked.

"It is obvious, Watson. Bauer knew the killer. Whether he was actually aware that the person is a murderer is moot. He clearly left his bed to come down to talk to him." Holmes gestured at the body. "No-one would chose to go outside to speak to a stranger clad in their nightclothes."

"Surely he must have realized that he was also in danger?" I asked.

Holmes shook his head, and lowered his voice so that only Lestrade and I could hear, "The man was a German agent. I suspect that he felt that he was untouchable."

Lestrade looked down at the corpse. "He's been touched, all right. About four times in the back with a sharp knife." Lestrade's tone was sour. He looked at Holmes. "I mucked up. I admit that. What can we do to salvage the situation? If we can."

Holmes frowned down at the remains of Otto Bauer. "I shall need to talk to Wiggins and see if he, or one of the other Irregulars saw anything." He looked up at me. "Watson, go back out onto the street and see if you can spot one of the boys, would you? One of them should be hanging around, they were, after all, watching Bauer for me."

I nodded and threaded my way back up the alley and out onto Whitefriars Street. A sizable crowd had gathered drawn, as always, by the excitement of grisly death. In many ways the London mob had not changed from those that had gathered outside Newgate to witness hangings, or, centuries earlier, had clustered around the gibbet at Tyburn, munching on pies and catcalling the condemned.

Looking around I spotted Wiggins, who had managed to push himself to the front of the crowd. I nodded to him, and beckoned, and he shot across the road, swerving to avoid the police constable who had a grab at him. I placed my hand on the lad's shoulder and steered him into the alley before the constable could say anything.

Wiggins took one look at the corpse and swore pungently. I, with my military background, could not help being impressed by the range and profanity of the lad's language. Old sweat sergeants and corporals would have been amazed and awed by Wiggins's turn of phrase.

Wiggins looked up at Holmes. "Cove got 'ome about ten last night. Went in the front door an' didn't come out again." He glared at the corpse as if it had personally offended him. "Couldn't keep watch on the back. Bloody beat copper ran Timmy off. Said he'd fling 'im in the watch 'ouse if 'e caught 'im around 'ere again. Tweren't nothin' we could do, guvnor."

"Where did he go before he came home?" Lestrade asked.

"Yesterdee afternoon 'e went to St. James Park. Fed the ducks. "Oo does that? Waste good food on bleedin' birds? Bloody barmy if you ask me. 'Ad to leave 'im in the park. None o' us are dressed for a posh park an' a couple o' toffs was givin' me an' Toby the eye, like they thought we was gonna dip 'em."

"Dip them?" I looked to Lestrade for clarification.

It was Holmes who responded. "Pick their pockets, Watson."

Wiggins nodded. "Right insultin' it was. We don't do that. Don't need to. The guvnor 'ere pays us good for the work we does. Anyway, we waits outside the park till 'e comes out again and we follows 'im."

"Where did he go?" Lestrade asked.

Wiggins rolled his eyes. "Back down the bleeding docks again. 'E was a bugger to follow. 'E got a cab just outside the park. You ever run after a cab for miles? We was bloody knackered. 'E 'ung around the docks for a bit, then came back 'ere. Went inside an' that's the last any o' us seen o' 'im."

"Thank you, Wiggins," Holmes said gravely. He took a handful of coins from his pocket and passed them to the lad. Wiggins grinned cheerfully and tucked the money away inside his shirt.

"Watson, would you be so kind as to escort Wiggins back out onto the street. Just in case any of the officers there get a little overzealous?"

"Ain't necessary, guvnor." Wiggins's grin got wider. "Ain't a bleedin' copper 'oo can catch me."

He gave a sloppy salute and then shot down the alley and out into the street. I followed him to make sure that he was all right. Wiggins dodged three cantankerous constables and disappeared down the road towards Fleet Street. I chuckled to myself and I rejoined Holmes and Lestrade.

Holmes was looking around the small rear yard. "It is obvious that whoever our killer is that he lured Bauer outside."

"How can you know that?" Lestrade asked.

Holmes pointed to the scattering of small pebbles that I had noticed. "Those do not come from this yard. Look around you, Lestrade, there is no source for them. Our killer came into the yard and threw a handful of pebbles at Bauer's window to get his attention." He pointed up at the face of the building. All but one of the windows were closed and, no doubt, latched securely.

Lestrade blinked. "How can you tell which window was Bauer's?"

Holmes shot Lestrade an irritated look. "Really, Lestrade, you are not usually this dense. The window that is open is obviously Bauer's. He opened it when the pebbles rattled against it."

"It is Bauer's room," Lestrade admitted, "I have already spoken with the landlord and he showed me the room. But you cannot know that Bauer opened the window because someone threw gravel at it. Maybe he slept with it open."

Holmes snorted. "That is extremely unlikely, Lestrade. In this part of London, not only do you have to deal with the smell from the river, but an open window is an invitation to burglary, as you well know."

Lestrade grudgingly nodded his agreement with Holmes's assessment.

Holmes continued, "Bauer came down to talk with his killer. Although on further reflection I do not think he realized that his interlocutor was a murderer."

"Why not, Holmes?" I asked.

"He turned his back on him, Watson. Would you turn your back on a murderer? Moreover one whose method of killing is to stab into the kidneys? Bauer knew about the killings and the method because, if you recall, I told him myself yesterday. Therefore, he did not believe that the man he was speaking with was the murderer."

"That is four men he has stabbed in the back," I observed. "The killer must seem to be extremely trustworthy to them. They were not expecting to die."

Lestrade grunted. "If murderers looked like they did in the Police Gazette or the Illustrated Police News catching them would be a lot easier."

Lestrade's acid comment bore witness to the exaggerated style of both publications in which killers always seemed to be drawn as brooding and menacing. The sort of men you would cross the road to avoid and certainly would not turn your back on in any circumstances.

Lestrade looked at Holmes. "Do you wish to accompany the body to the morgue?"

Holmes shook his head. "I very much doubt the corpse has anything of interest to tell us. But I would like to examine Bauer's room."

Lestrade signaled to the constables to remove the corpse. There was nothing untoward on the steps beneath the body so we went in to the building via the rear entrance, rather than braving the curious crowds at the front of the building.

Bauer's landlord was a nervous little man whose hands fluttered in an agitated manner like trapped butterflies, as he showed us up the stairs to the room that Otto Bauer had occupied.

The room was reasonably spacious for a single room lodging. There was a comfortable looking bed resting beneath the open window. A gleam of white porcelain showed that a new chamber pot rested beneath the bed. At the foot of the bed sat a blanket box.

Against the wall next to the bed sat an old oaken chest of drawers, much scratched and scuffed with age and hard usage, with a cheap porcelain washing bowl and ewer resting on top of it. Beside the bowl sat a few oddments; loose coins and keys. The sort of things a man takes from his pockets at the end of the day.

There were no pictures of any sort upon the walls nor any mementos of his home in Germany. In short, the room lacked any sort of character and gave no indications as to the personality of its late occupant.

I thought my friend was hoping to discover papers that would link Bauer to the other murdered men and to the German government, but when I mentioned this to Holmes he simply shook his head.

"Criminals may write things down, my dear Watson, but spies never do. Bauer's orders would most likely have been word of mouth only."

A search of the room proved my friend to be correct. Details pertaining to a local bank account were found in a drawer, but a perusal of them showed that Bauer had had no more money than one would expect a single clerk working for a reasonably prosperous wine merchant to have.

The bed box yielded only spare bedding and clothing, and there was nothing in the chest of drawers apart from a few starched and rolled collars organized with almost regimental precision, and a scattering of neatly folded woollen vests and pants. There were no letters from home, something that I found odd and said so.

Holmes nodded thoughtfully. "I suspect that Mr. Bauer wanted to keep anything of value away from the prying eyes of his landlord." He eyed the keys sitting atop the chest of drawers.

"Could he have kept anything at his place of work?" Lestrade asked.

"Very likely, Lestrade. Come, it is time we paid Mr. Rutherford another visit." Holmes picked up the keys, placed them in his pocket, and walked towards the door, then stopped and turned to Lestrade. "Has Rutherford been advised that his employee is deceased?"

Lestrade nodded. "Mr. Rutherford sent for the police when Bauer did not arrive at work. He said it was unlike the man. The sergeant who spoke to him was aware that Bauer was of interest to me and sent a constable to fetch me. We came straight here." He glanced out of the window. "Well, you know what we found."

"Quite," Holmes said softly. He turned back to the door. After a moment Lestrade and I followed him.

We walked from Bauer's lodgings to his place of employment in silence. The bell that jingled merrily over the door as we entered Rutherford and Sons seemed to me to be completely out of place. I noted that Lestrade winced at the merry peal, so he no doubt felt the same as I did. Holmes did not appear to have even noticed the bell.

Josiah Rutherford came out of a back room. He was composed, though pale, and I noted that he had already placed a mourning band around the upper part of his right arm.

"A sad morning, gentlemen," he greeted us. "Am I to assume that you wish to see whatever private belongings that Otto kept here."

"If it is not too much of an imposition," Lestrade replied.

Rutherford sighed. "I will have to clean his desk out anyway when I hire a new clerk. It would be best if you take anything you need with you. His private papers should really go back to his family in Germany, I suppose, but I have no idea what family he had."

"Someone at the German embassy should be able to assist you with that," Lestrade said.

"An excellent idea, Inspector, thank you."

Rutherford led us behind the counter and into a small room, little larger that a cupboard. A writing desk sat with a straight chair tucked under it. It was situated in such a way that the person at the desk could see out into the shop.

Holmes sorted through the keys that he had taking from Bauer's room and found the one to fit the lock on the desk.

Holmes riffled through the desk. He opened several books. "I see Bauer did your accounts for you, Mr. Rutherford."

"He did indeed, Mr. Holmes. He was very thorough. The books were never out by so much as a farthing," Rutherford replied.

Holmes set one book aside and looked at Rutherford. "I should like to take this to examine."

Rutherford raised an eyebrow. "You think that Otto may have been thieving from me? I assure you Mr. Holmes, that Otto Bauer was as honest as the day is long."

"That is as may be," Holmes replied. "But Bauer was working on this book recently. I would like to be sure that nothing connected to his employment could have caused his death."

"How do you know that he worked on that book recently?" I asked. I gestured to the other ledgers and a sprinkling of order books that lay inside the desk.

Holmes flicked the book open and showed it to me. "The entries are dated, though I agree that could be faked. However, the brightness and clarity of the ink tells me that these entries are the most recent." He picked up another ledger and opened it to show me how the ink was fading on earlier entries.

"I really should do a monograph on the possibilities inherent in the study of various inks. It could prove to be particularly useful in the fields of crime detection, especially those of fraud, embezzlement, and blackmail," Holmes commented.

Holmes hummed to himself as he methodically removed everything from the desk. He made a sound of satisfaction as a bundle of papers came to light. It was about six inches thick and tied up with red legal ribbon. Holmes untied this and flicked through the papers. "Written in German, understandable, as it was his native tongue."

"Can you read them?" Lestrade asked.

Holmes shook his head. "I have a little German, as you know…"

I smiled slightly at the reference to our first case together.

"…but not enough to get the subtle nuances of the correspondence."

Holmes tied the papers back up, and tucked the ledger under his arm. He turned to Mr. Rutherford. "We shall get the ledger back to you as soon as possible, Mr. Rutherford."

"I appreciate that, Mr. Holmes." Rutherford looked around the shop and sighed again. "It is going to be dashed awkward doing business without a competent clerk. Bauer wasn't an easy man to get to know, or even particularly likeable, but he was extremely competent."

We took our leave of the wine merchant and went out into the street.

"Where to now, Mr. Holmes?" asked Lestrade. "I really should follow up on the corpse. Not expecting any surprises at the post-mortem, but it is probably best that I attend."

Holmes nodded. "Watson and I will go back to Baker Street. I will send a message to my brother. He can send someone to take the letters. He will know someone who will be able to translate them properly. Mycroft can also have the ledger after I have examined it. If there is anything odd in the books, his people will find it."

Chapter Nineteen

Once back at Baker Street a telegram was sent to Mycroft. About an hour later a man I recognized as Mycroft's clerk arrived to collect the letters.

Holmes spent the afternoon poring over Rutherford and Sons' latest ledger.

I settled in for the afternoon with a recently purchased book: "A Tale of the House of the Wolfings" by William Morris. It had received such a marvelous review from Oscar Wilde in the Pall Mall Gazette that I was keen to read it.

It was heading on towards dusk before Holmes finally shut the ledger and sat back from his desk.

"Well, we can be certain of one thing, my dear Watson," he said.

"And that is?" I asked.

"Whatever Bauer was doing he was taking care not to compromise Rutherford and Sons. The ledger seems fairly straightforward. No unusually large amounts of money went through the books recently. Nothing that cannot be accounted for, at any rate." Holmes frowned down at the ledger. "Though I may still give the ledger to Mycroft for his examination."

I raised my eyebrows. "You think you may have missed something?"

Holmes gave a bark of humourless laughter. "No indeed, I am fairly certain that there is nothing nefarious contained in the ledger, but sometimes a second pair of eyes is a good thing."

Our conversation was halted by Mrs. Hudson coming in to our rooms escorting a well-dressed, stiff-backed gentleman, with the blank expression of a well-trained servant. He clicked his heels in the Prussian manner, and extended a stiff, cream-coloured envelope to Holmes. "Herr Holmes, I presume?"

Holmes rose from his seat. "I am he."

"This is for you, Herr. Holmes, and also Herr Doktor." He nodded at me.

Holmes took the proffered envelope and proceeded to slit it open with his jack-knife which he wrenched out of the mantelpiece where it kept his unopened correspondence pinned in place.

The man did not so much as blink at Holmes' actions.

Holmes jabbed the knife back into the mantelpiece and extracted a sheet of paper from the envelope. He scanned the contents for a moment before looking up at the messenger.

"Pray tell the ambassador that we will call upon him at the requested time."

"Very good, Herr Holmes." The man clicked his heels again, turned smartly, and marched out of our rooms. Holmes shut the door behind him.

"The ambassador?" I asked, for want of something to say.

"We have been invited to call upon Paul von Hatzfeldt, German Ambassador, at the embassy in Carlton House Terrace at 11 o'clock tomorrow morning."

"Just you and me?"

Holmes shook his head, and held the invitation so that I could see that it bore three names. "Our good Inspector Lestrade is invited to join us."

"Do you wish me to send Lestrade a telegram?" I asked.

Holmes shook his head. "I think not. Come Watson, get your coat. We shall call at Scotland Yard and collect Lestrade, and then go on to the Diogenes Club. The time has come for another discussion with Mycroft."

Holmes shrugged himself in to his coat, took out the carefully wrapped gun and placed it in his pocket, placed the invitation in the inside pocket of his coat, and tucked the ledger under one arm.

I had been looking forward to my dinner and was not happy at the prospect of going out.

Holmes knew my expressions from old. "What say you to supper at Simpson's, hmmm?"

I laughed and got to my feet. "I never say no to supper at Simpson's."

Lestrade was still in his office at Scotland Yard when we arrived. He was only too pleased to leave and join us in the short walk to the Diogenes Club. Lestrade was even happier than I was at the idea of supper at Simpson's afterwards.

Once at the Diogenes we were shown into the Stranger's Room, and an usher was dispatched to locate Mycroft.

We had barely made ourselves comfortable when Mycroft Holmes came into the room. He looked at his brother with raised eyebrows, "This is unusual, Sherlock, normally you would send a message. Has something happened?"

"I am sure that by now your agents have informed you of the murders of both Robert Glasheen and Otto Bauer," Holmes replied.

Mycroft made a noise that could be taken as agreement, as he sat in his chair. "Something else has happened."

It was a statement not a question.

"It has," Holmes confirmed. He took the invitation from his pocket and handed it to Mycroft, who studied it for a moment before handing it back.

"You must go, of course," Mycroft said.

Holmes nodded. "I confirmed our acceptance."

Lestrade shook his head. "I am at a loss as to what the German Ambassador wants with the likes of us."

"That is simple, Inspector," Mycroft said. "He wants to know how much you know about the putative supply of guns by his masters."

"Not putative anymore," Holmes said. He took the carefully wrapped gun from his pocket and handed it to Mycroft.

Mycroft unwrapped the bundle and stared at the contents.

"You know what it is, of course," said Holmes.

"Of course I do, Sherlock," Mycroft replied. "It is a M1879 Reichsrevolver." He looked at his brother. "Where did you get this?"

"It was found in the room of the late Robert Glasheen," Holmes replied. "A man who certainly had no business owning such a weapon."

"And this Glasheen worked at Duncran Wharf?" asked Mycroft.

"He did," replied Holmes. "And according to his sister he was a member of Clan na Gael. Though he apparently was not readily trusted on account of the sister being married to an Englishman, and a policeman at that."

"Can we link Robert Glasheen to Otto Bauer?" asked Mycroft.

It was Lestrade who replied, "We can, but it is not the sort of evidence I would want to build a case out of. The two men were seen talking together. That is all."

Mycroft shook his head. "Not nearly enough. Besides which, I need a live Clan na Gael member who will talk. A dead one is of no use."

"What about the letters Holmes found? I asked. "Were they of any interest?"

"They were most definitely of interest, Doctor Watson," Mycroft replied. "We believe them to be in code."

"A cypher?" queried Holmes.

Mycroft shook his head. "No. Straight forward enough. Letters in cypher would be too obvious if intercepted. These letters are to and from Bauer and an alleged friend in Germany who is supposedly courting. Bauer kept copies of his replies so we could see the progression of the correspondence quite easily."

Something Mycroft said made me stop and think. "Supposedly courting?" I asked, wondering how Mycroft had come to that conclusion.

"The letters discuss a Fraulein Weisskapelle, whom the writer in Germany is supposedly courting. Discussing gifts to woo her and such like," Mycroft said.

Lestrade frowned at Mycroft. "But you don't think the lady exists, do you?

"I do not, Inspector, and neither do the people who translated the letters. In the first instance it is the young lady's name that gives pause for thought."

"Why?" I asked.

"Because, doctor, Weisskapelle, translated into English becomes Whitechapel," replied Mycroft.

"I suppose calling her Miss London Docks would have been just a little too obvious," observed Lestrade.

"Indeed, Inspector," Mycroft said, his tone slightly acidic. "We do know that some members of Clan na Gael are based in Whitechapel. However, it is the final letter in the bundle that proved to be the most interesting."

"What did it say?" asked Holmes.

"It was a copy of the last letter that Bauer had written. In it he stated that in his opinion it would be best if his friend ceased plying Miss Whitechapel with gifts, as they were obviously not appreciated and were clearly going astray."

Lestrade whistled. "Well now, that is interesting."

I looked at Lestrade in some slight confusion. Holmes noticed and took pity on me. "The gifts to Miss Whitechapel, my dear Watson, are the guns."

This made sense to me. "So Otto Bauer had recommended to his superiors that no more guns be supplied to Clan na Gael. No wonder he was murdered."

"Say nothing of this to the ambassador, tomorrow, gentlemen, please. Her Majesty's government would prefer Paul von Hatzfeldt to be kept in the dark a little longer," said Mycroft.

"Giving him enough rope to hang himself with, eh?" said Lestrade.

"One rarely hangs diplomats, Lestrade," Holmes said. "It is not considered the gentlemanly thing to do."

Chapter Twenty

The following morning we arrived at the German Embassy at Prussia House in Carlton House Terrace just before the invited time of 11 o'clock, to find Lestrade already waiting for us.

The little detective would not own to being nervous about the forthcoming meeting, but he was bouncing on the balls of his feet and his moustache was perceptibly twitching. A nervous Lestrade was one who was more rodent-like than was usual. I realized that this sort of visit was well outside the realms of Lestrade's experience, and if I were to be honest with myself, it was out of mine as well.

Holmes, however, seemed completely relaxed, as if he hobnobbed with dignitaries every day. Though to be fair, given his extensive clientele, more than a few people of rank and title had passed through our flat in search of assistance.

At precisely 11 o'clock we entered the embassy and were met by the man who had delivered the invitation to Baker Street the previous day.

He greeted us courteously and escorted us into what was clearly the ambassador's office. Four chairs, and a pair of exquisite lacquered occasional tables, sat close to a marble fireplace that would have been the focal point of the room, if not for the ornate mahogany desk that dominated the room and drew your eyes as you entered.

The ambassador, who was sitting behind the desk as we entered, rose to his feet, came and shook our hands and showed us to the comfortable looking seats before the fire place.

Paul von Hatzfeldt, or to give him his full name, Melchior Hubert Paul Gustav Graf von Hatzfeldt zu Wildenburg, was the Kaiser's ambassador to London. He was a tall, thin, man, with an oval face, even features, a receding hairline, and a moustache that was even more opulent than Lestrade's. He had been described by noted German statesman, Otto von Bismarck as, "The best horse in the diplomatic stable".

As we seated ourselves, the flunky returned, pushing a tea-trolley leaden with fine china cups, saucers and plates, a steaming teapot, and a fine array of cakes and delicate sandwiches.

The ambassador poured us each a cup. "I find the English habit of discussing business over a cup of tea and a few comestibles to be an extremely civilized one," von Hatzfeldt said, as he handed out the cups and gestured to us to help ourselves to food.

After taking a sip or two of tea, von Hatzfeldt put his cup down and turned to Lestrade. "I am concerned, Inspector, that Scotland Yard's hounding of my countryman has led to his death."

Lestrade opened his mouth to reply, but Holmes laid a gentle hand upon his arm and shook his head.

"You have been misinformed, Your Excellency," Holmes said softly.

The ambassador's eyebrows rose. "I have? Then pray, Mr. Holmes, enlighten me."

"Otto Bauer brought his own death upon himself. He was going to places and consorting with people that, if he were an honest man, he should not have been," said Holmes.

"And how do you arrive at that conclusion, Mr. Holmes?"

"The manner of Bauer's death," Holmes replied.

"He was stabbed, I believe," said von Hatzfeldt.

Holmes nodded. "In the back, as he turned to reenter his lodging house after leaving his room to talk to his killer."

The ambassador was silent for a moment. "You know this for a fact, Mr. Holmes?"

"I do, Your Excellency. Otto Bauer was lured out of his room."

"You can prove this?"

"Otto Bauer was already in bed when his killer called. The man threw gravel at the window of Bauer's room, when Bauer opened the window and saw who it was, he went downstairs and out into the rear yard to meet him."

Holmes smiled briefly and without humour. "Bauer was wearing only his nightshirt and slippers when found. There are only three reasons a man would reasonably leave a house clad only in his night attire. One is fire; of which there was none. Two is to answer the call of nature; there was a chamber pot beneath the bed for that. The third is a clandestine meeting. In short, Your Excellency, Otto Bauer's death is not due to any perceived persecution by Scotland Yard. He trusted the wrong man."

Paul von Hatzfeldt was silent for a moment. "You are correct, Mr. Holmes. It does indeed appear that Herr Bauer's death was not of Scotland Yard's making." He turned to Lestrade. "My apologies, Inspector, if I offended."

"No offense taken, Your Excellency," Lestrade replied.

The ambassador turned back to Holmes. "Do you have any expectation of catching the killer? Many men carry knives in the course of their employment, do they not? Butchers, dock workers, and skinners all come to mind."

Holmes rose to his feet, his face unreadable. "Rest assured, Your Excellency, the killer will be caught."

Paul von Hatzfeldt inclined his head graciously. "It pleases me to hear that, Mr. Holmes."

We took our leave of the ambassador and walked out of the embassy. We paused on the steps to allow our eyes to adjust to the light after the relative dimness of the interior of the building.

As we stood there, I heard a noise that I had not heard for some time, and certainly did not expect to hear in the middle of London: the sharp crack of a revolver being fired. Without thinking I hurled myself at Holmes, taking him to the ground in a tackle that would have cheered the hearts of my former rugby teammates at Blackheath.

We rolled into the shelter of the building's portico. Lestrade drew his own revolver and stood guard over us both, while shouting orders at those passing to take shelter, and to curious embassy workers to get back inside.

Paul von Hatzfeldt himself came out, his countenance a blaze of fury. He helped Holmes and I to our feet and swiftly escorted us back into the embassy. Lestrade came behind us, only putting his gun away when the door was safely locked behind us.

Holmes waved off the offer of brandy for shock, but did accept the ambassador's offer of his private coach to take us back to Baker Street.

We had not been long home when Mycroft arrived. It was unlike Mycroft to break his daily routines. His face was anxious as I opened the door to him.

"Is he all right, Doctor Watson?"

I realized that whoever had witnessed the incident at the embassy and informed Mycroft must not have been able to tell whether or not Holmes had actually been shot, thereby causing Mycroft Holmes not a little distress.

"I am in excellent health, Mycroft," Holmes assured his brother from where he reclined upon the couch, "I have a few bruises from where my good Watson thumped me into the ground, but apart from that I am remarkably unscathed."

"I am relieved to hear it, Sherlock," Mycroft replied, seating himself in a chair beside the couch.

Mycroft looked towards where Lestrade was leaning against the mantelpiece. "I understand that you stood guard over my brother and Doctor Watson."

Lestrade shrugged. "I had a gun. They did not. Nor could we know if another shot would be taken. If the assailant had shot again, perhaps I could have got him."

Mycroft inclined his head. "Perhaps. My agent was not able to identify the shooter beyond to say it was a man who ran down Carlton House Terrace and onto Pall Mall."

"Pall Mall, eh?" said Lestrade. "Is it possible that the shooter was a German agent? That he slipped into the embassy by a rear entrance?"

"That is unlikely, Inspector," said Mycroft. "Such an act could easily be interpreted as an act of war, if Her Majesty's government chose to treat it as such. At the moment the German government does not want all-out war, no matter what the Kaiser thinks of the English."

"Mycroft is correct," said Holmes. "We are getting a little too close to the killer, so he decided to remove me."

"But it was a gun," I blurted. "The other killings were a knife."

"Oh Watson," Holmes said, shaking his head. "Think, man. Do you honestly believe I would turn my back on anyone I did not know? The victims have all been killed by someone they know and, to a degree, trusted."

A strange thought came into my mind. I wondered if the killer could be Michael Geraghty himself. A man who must have been trusted by most, if not all, the victims. And we only had his word for it that he was not involved with Clan na Gael.

Before I could say anything, however, Mycroft got to his feet.

"I am glad that you are unharmed, Sherlock. But are you any closer to the killer?"

"Thank you, Mycroft. I do believe that I am. The ambassador was very helpful."

"He was?" I blinked at Holmes, then looked at Lestrade, who looked as mystified as myself.

"I have said before, my friend, that you see but you do not observe," said Holmes. "I could equally have said you hear, but you do not listen."

He closed his eyes, refusing to comment any further, leaving me to show Mycroft and Lestrade to the door.

Chapter Twenty One

It was two days before things came to a head. Holmes had spent the two days going over all the evidence he had collected. He seemed to have reached a conclusion, but when I asked him, he merely shook his head. "Not yet, my dear Watson. I still do not have all the pieces to the puzzle. Tomorrow you and I and Lestrade shall pay a man a visit, then, after that, all being well, Lestrade will be able to arrest a murderer."

Holmes arranged for us to meet with Lestrade the next day at the Yard, and we took a cab from there into Whitechapel. Holmes directed the cabby to take us to the police station on Leman Street, so there were no clues to be had to our ultimate destination.

The station was in something of a tumult when we arrived. Inspector Reid was standing in the street talking to several well-dressed gentlemen, who had the look of bankers or prosperous businessmen to them, and who consequently looked extremely out of place.

Inspector Reid saw us get down from the cab, and saying something to the men, crossed the road to greet us.

"This is a timely arrival, gentlemen," Reid said. "I was about to send a constable to Scotland Yard. Have you heard of the murder already?"

Holmes shook his head. "No. Indeed, I was hoping to prevent one. I take it that James Harrison has been murdered?"

Reid gaped at him for a moment. "How did you know that Harrison had been murdered?"

"I did not. The presence of so many well-dressed gentlemen, several of whom have been in the newspapers complaining about the dock strike, tells me that someone attached to the docks has been killed. You would not get such a turnout for a labourer, therefore someone a little further up the chain has been killed. But not too far up the chain. If that had been the case, they would have gone straight to Scotland Yard, rather than come to Leman Street."

Reid scratched at the back of his head, his expression rueful. "It seems so simple when you explain it, Mr. Holmes, but it's downright uncanny all the same. Perhaps you would care to have a word with these gents?" He gestured at the knot of men who were looking at us with something approaching puzzlement mixed in with annoyance.

"Of course," Holmes said, and began to walk across the road to the men.

I hastened alongside him. "Holmes," I said softly, "Were you expecting Harrison to be killed?"

Holmes shook his head. "No, Watson, I was not. I did not believe him to be involved in this except peripherally in his capacity of bribing Tyler to keep Duncran Wharf from working."

"Then why was he killed?" I asked.

"That, my friend, is what we need to discover," Holmes replied.

Inspector Reid introduced us to the men from the London and St. Katherine's Docks Company, who, once introduced to Holmes, seemed to be quite pleased that my friend was taking an interest in the case. One of their number was sent to escort us to where Harrison's body lay, in a dark alleyway close by the gates to the London Docks.

James Harrison lay face down on the cobblestones. A brief examination showed me that he had been stabbed in the kidneys, the same as the other victims. But try as I might, I could not see how James Harrison could be linked to Clan na Gael and the machinations of the German government.

Lestrade was obviously having the same problem, because he asked "Could this be the work of the gang that Harrison was in debt to?"

Holmes snorted his derision at the suggestion. "Come now, Lestrade, you know as well as I do that stabbing in such a fashion is not how those gangs work. If a gang had been involved Harrison would have been beaten up and then tossed into the river. Whether he was dead or alive when he went in would have been up to the police surgeon to determine."

Lestrade nodded, his expression sour, acknowledging the truth of Holmes's words.

Holmes looked at the London Docks lackey who had accompanied us. He was a skinny, nervous looking man, who seemed to find the company of two police detectives, and a renowned consulting detective and his biographer doctor, a little too exciting for his taste. The man jumped like a startled flea any time any one of us so much as looked at to him.

"Who found the corpse?" Holmes asked.

"One of the men who had been watching the gates overnight, Mr. Holmes. Jack Miller. He found the body when he was leaving." The man's voice was little more than a thin squeak.

"Is he available to speak with?" Reid asked.

The man nodded. "We kept him at the gatehouse. The managers thought that the police would want to speak with him." He paused, and swallowed convulsively. "I must warn you, Mr. Miller isn't happy about staying behind. He was complaining quite loudly about wanting his breakfast and his bed."

"I can understand that," Lestrade commented, in the tone of a man who fully comprehends the situation. "Working at night is not pleasant at any time."

Reid gestured to the uniformed constables who had accompanied us to wrap up the body for delivery to the police surgeon, and we followed our rather twitchy guide to the gatehouse at the London Docks.

Jack Miller, known to Holmes and, no doubt, others as Jacky Roundhouse, was clearly not happy, though his grumbling ceased when he spotted Holmes.

"Just tell us what you saw, Jacky, and you can go," Holmes said.

Jacky scratched at the back of his head. "It were real odd, Mr. 'Olmes. It was kinda quiet all night. The picketers tend to doze off round midnight. Their womenfolk havin' all gone 'ome to bed. Not necessarily their own, mind you."

"When did you last see Mr. Harrison?" Reid asked. "Alive," he added, seeing the slight gleam of mischief in Miller's eye.

"That would've been around ten. Mr. 'Arrison 'ad bin workin' late. I let 'im out the gates meself."

"Did you see him speak to anyone?" asked Lestrade.

"One o' the Blehane brothers from Duncran. Couldn't tell which one. It was near full dark by then and the lights at the gates ain't too bright."

"Did you see anyone else?" Holmes asked.

Jacky shrugged. "Just a woman. Probably some poor cow on the game fer a few pennies for a bed at the doss 'ouse. There's always plenty o' dollymops around o' a night."

"Where did you see her?" asked Holmes.

"She came past the alley and went up towards Whitechapel."

"Passed the alley or out of it?" Holmes asked softly.

Jacky shrugged again. "Could bin either, Mr. 'Olmes. As I said, the light weren't real good." He frowned. "There's somethin' I don't understand."

"What is that, Jacky?" asked Holmes.

"'Ow come I didn't 'ear Mr. 'Arrison scream? Bein' stabbed like that must've 'urt like billy-oh."

"And that is why," I said.

Jacky looked at me, his face creased in puzzlement.

"The pain is so intense," I explained, "that the person stabbed cannot make a sound."

Jacky's face cleared and a grin spread across it, "Like when yer, accidentally like, punch a cove in the tallywags? Sort o' makes a whooshin' noise an' a squeak, but that's all."

"Exactly," I said, struggling to keep my face straight.

"Well," Jacky said, "Don't that beat all?" He looked at Holmes. "Anythin' else, Mr. 'Olmes?"

Holmes looked at Reid and Lestrade, who both shook their heads. "I do not think so, Jacky. Go get your breakfast and some sleep, you have earned it."

Holmes handed Jacky a sovereign. The man grinned delightedly, closing his fist tightly around the coin. "A decent breakfast fer me fer once! I fancy a bite o' bacon an' sausages. Thanks Mr. 'Olmes. You're a real gent."

He saluted Holmes, including the rest of us in the gesture, before slipping out the door. We could hear him whistling his way down the dock towards the gates.

"Well, Holmes?" said Lestrade, eyebrows raised in query.

"Come gentlemen," Holmes said, "It is time that we paid another visit to the Geraghtys." He walked out of the gatehouse leaving us to stare blankly at each other for a moment, before hastening after the departing Holmes.

"Why visit the Geraghty family again, Holmes?" I asked. I was wondering if Holmes suspected Michael Geraghty was the killer, as I had begun to.

"The family is the key to all this, Watson," Holmes replied gnomically, and then refused to say anything else.

Chapter Twenty Two

We strode silently through the teaming streets of Whitechapel. The noise of the inhabitants flowed around us, but I doubt any of us really heard what was been shouted by the street vendors.

Holmes was fixed on our destination, I was lost in wondering if I was correct in my suspicions about Michael Geraghty, and God alone knew what was occupying the minds of Inspectors Lestrade and Reid, but they both wore looks of grim determination.

When we arrived at the Geraghty house, Holmes stepped up to the door and knocked briskly. The door was opened by Mrs. Geraghty herself, an apron tied around her waist and her hair bound up in a scarf. From the noises coming from inside it was clearly laundry day and every hand to the pumps.

"Good morning, Mrs. Geraghty," said Holmes. "Is Michael available to speak with?"

"Here he comes now, Holmes," said Lestrade, pointing up the street to where Michael Geraghty and William Blehane were approaching from the opposite direction.

Mrs. Geraghty stared at her son. "What are you doing here? And with William?"

"What do you mean?" Michael Geraghty asked his mother.

"Peter came here not ten minutes ago, saying William had sent him to fetch Julia to meet you both at the wharf."

Holmes whirled around, "Quickly! There is no time to waste!" He started to stride down the street.

Reid called after him. "Whatever is wrong, Mr. Holmes?"

"Miss Geraghty has just gone for a stroll with a murderer, inspector," Holmes shot back over his shoulder. "I think we should stop that, do you not agree?"

Michael Geraghty ran to Holmes's side. "Peter's the killer? Peter killed John and the others?"

"He did, Mr. Geraghty. Peter Blehane is, I suspect, a member of Clan na Gael." Holmes looked around at us, not breaking stride, "Are you gentlemen coming with us, or not?"

Lestrade, Reid and I hastened to follow, sweeping a stunned William Blehane along in our wake.

As we pushed our way through the streets of Whitechapel, ignoring the abuse hurled at us by passersby, a small figure slid out of an alley and up to Holmes. It was Wiggins. I was surprised to see the lad. As far as I was aware his part in this affair had ended when Otto Bauer was murdered.

"I bin keepin' an eye on the Mick's 'ouse," he said to Holmes. "Figgered yer'd want to know 'oo came an' went, like."

Reid raised an eyebrow. "Who is this enterprising lad?"

"This, Inspector Reid, is Wiggins, the leader of my Baker Street Irregulars," Holmes replied. He looked at Wiggins. "What happened this morning, Wiggins?"

"Not much," the lad admitted. He nodded at William Blehane, "Until 'is brother turned up. Chatted to the girl on the step then they went off up the street together."

"To Duncran Wharf," I said.

Wiggins shook his head. "Nah. They ain't goin' there. That's why I stopped yer. They headed fer King 'Enry's Steps."

"Why on earth...?" I started to ask.

Reid swore. "Watermen of somewhat dubious reputation ply their trade at the bottom of those steps, Doctor Watson. You want to get to a boat on the river unseen, then they will get you there. But it will cost you. And they don't care if one of the passengers is unwilling."

"Peter Blehane is abducting my sister?" Michael Geraghty roared. "We'll see about that, by God!"

He started running and we all had to run to keep up with him as the furious man pushed people out of his way as he hastened to his sister's rescue.

King Henry's Steps were very old. They had an older name that was not much used any more. They had been known as Execution Dock Steps and led down to the strip of the Thames river bank known as Execution Dock.

Ahead of us we could see two figures almost at the top of the somewhat rickety steps. Michael Geraghty roared out Peter Blehane's name, causing both figures to swing around and stare at him.

Peter then seized Julia Geraghty around the waist, holding her close to his side. He produced one of the German revolvers from his pocket and aimed it roughly in our direction.

"No closer," Peter Blehane yelled. "Or I will shoot her!"

William, who had been running towards them, slowed to a halt, grasping Michael's arm to stop him as well.

William raised his hands in a placating gesture. "Please, brother, let my sweet Julia go."

Peter spat on the ground besides Julia's skirts. "You're no brother o' mine. Kissing the arse o' the English, with nary a concern for our homeland, imprisoned as it is in the chains of English slavery."

"Like me, Peter, you were born here," William said softly. "London is our home."

Peter Blehane opened his mouth to reply, then suddenly screamed in pain.

Julia Geraghty had plucked a pin from her hair and had jabbed it hard into Peter Blehane's hand.

Hair tumbling free around her shoulders in a lopsided manner, as her chignon collapsed with the removal of the hairpin, she wrenched herself from Peter Blehane's grasp. The hairpin fell from her hand and tumbled down the stairs to sink into the mud of the Thames below.

Julia Geraghty hurled herself into William's arms and buried her face in his shoulder. His arms tightened around her protectively. Michael placed himself between them and Peter Blehane, glaring furiously at the man, making it clearly obvious that if the man wanted to kill his sister he had to go through him first.

Lestrade and Reid stepped around the couple and their protector, running towards their quarry. Peter Blehane looked around wildly, seemingly trying to decide which police inspector to shoot first. They did not give him a chance. Both men took him down hard, almost rolling off the edge of the steps into the mud below.

Lestrade finally managed to handcuff Blehane and drag him to his feet. "Peter Blehane, I arrest you for the murders of John Geraghty, Jack Tyler, Robert Glasheen, Otto Bauer and James Harrison, as well as for the crimes of smuggling and sedition, not to mention the abduction of Miss Geraghty."

He and Inspector Reid dragged their prisoner, swearing furiously, away.

Chapter Twenty Three

Holmes and I returned to Baker Street. My friend was in a somber mood. There was none of the jubilation that so often followed the conclusion of a successful case.

I watched him with some concern. It was if, in his mind, the case were not yet over. But with the arrest of Peter Blehane, the murders were over. Indeed, Holmes had referred to Peter Blehane as the murderer, so why was he so grim?

"Holmes," I said. "There were so many deaths, and I do not understand why they were all killed."

"It is simplicity itself, my dear Watson."

"To you, perhaps, but to me all I see are dead men who had some loose association with their killer. And in the case of Harrison, I cannot see the link at all."

Holmes leaned forward and plucked his Persian slipper from the mantelpiece, and proceeded to fill his pipe. He lit it and sat back taking a meditative puff or two before speaking.

"We shall look at them in order, shall we?"

"If you please, Holmes," I replied.

"The first murder, and the one that brought Michael Geraghty to our door, was that of his brother John, found murdered in an alley behind the Ten Bells public house. That was the most straightforward killing. John Geraghty died because he had discovered that guns were being smuggled into London via Duncran Wharf."

I had taken out my notebook and was jotting everything down as Holmes spoke.

"The second death, that of Jack Tyler, is a little more complicated. Tyler was taking bribes from James Harrison to keep Duncran Wharf on strike until the Geraghty family were forced to sell it. That did not suit Peter Blehane. If the wharf was not working, then the guns were not coming in."

"That makes sense," I said. "What about Robert Glasheen's murder?"

"You remember Mycroft told us that German guns were turning up in the hands of London crooks?"

"Yes."

"Glasheen was the source. He was skimming off a few from each consignment and selling them. I suspect, though I cannot prove it, that he was selling the guns to help his family."

I thought back to the little shop in Wapping, and its general air of being rundown and neglected, and to Glasheen's comments about the vouchers to strikers not being properly honoured, leaving honest shopkeepers scraping for a living.

Holmes took another puff of his pipe, "Otto Bauer was killed because he advised his masters in Germany not to send any more guns. Remember the letter Mycroft spoke about to us?"

I nodded.

"I suspect that Peter Blehane went to Bauer to try and persuade him to change his mind. When Bauer would not, Blehane killed him."

"And James Harrison?" I asked.

"Peter Blehane was clearing the decks. Harrison was killed mostly because he bribed Tyler to keep the wharf on strike."

"You said this morning that you were hoping to prevent a murder."

"I did."

"Who did you think would be next, Harrison?"

Holmes shook his head. "I thought Michael Geraghty would be the target. Because he would not let the murder of his brother go. He not only got us involved, but Scotland Yard became involved as well."

"Holmes," I said as the thought struck me. "You said that the German Ambassador told you who the killer was!"

Holmes shook his head. "Not who, Watson, but what. Amongst those he listed as usually carrying knives were dock labourers. The ambassador was letting me know where to look for the killer."

I sat in silence for a while, thinking it all over. Finally I said, "I do not understand what Peter Blehane thought he would gain by abducting Miss Geraghty"

Holmes merely grunted and did not reply.

Several days later we were summoned to the Diogenes Club to meet with Mycroft. Lestrade was there waiting for us.

Mycroft waved us to seats and poured us all a whisky. "A toast, gentlemen, to the successful end to the case. Inspector Lestrade has a murderer, and I have a severely discommoded German Ambassador, and of even greater importance is the fact that there are no more German guns getting in the hands of London's undesirables."

Mycroft sipped his whisky and we all followed suit. "As to the remaining members of that group of Clan na Gael, a little discretion will be exercised."

"Oh?" Holmes enquired.

"We have decided, on this occasion, to let sleeping dogs lie. With Peter Blehane facing a trial that will almost certainly end with him being hanged, and with him being the mastermind of the affair, we have decided not to arrest any of the other possible members of the group. Of course, it goes without saying that we will be keeping a close eye on them."

"Of course," agreed Holmes.

"Dorothy will be kept busy," Lestrade observed.

"Indeed," I said. "There is much charitable work to be done in the East End."

Mycroft observed us all over the rim of his glass, but did not deign to reply.

Chapter Twenty Four

It was a few months later that I read in the morning papers that Peter Blehane had been hanged the previous day at Pentonville prison. His trial had garnered little interest, so little in fact, that I suspected that Mycroft had had a hand in suppressing it.

Therefore I was not surprised when we had a visitor later that same morning: Michael Geraghty.

"I came to thank you gentlemen for the effort you put in to find my brother's murderer. Though I own that I was not expecting to find such goings on as smuggling and sedition on my wharf," Michael Geraghty said.

Holmes waved a languid hand in acknowledgement but did not speak.

"What will you do now?" I asked.

"I have sold Duncran Wharf," Michael replied, much to my astonishment. "Though there was little enough about the affair in the papers, word gets around, and there was some anxiety about dealing with us." He paused and took a deep breath. "So I sold Duncran to the London and St. Katherine Docks Company, for considerably more than they originally offered."

"How on earth did you manage that?" I asked.

Michael Geraghty chuckled; a rich warm laugh. "I simply pointed out, Doctor, that people would be less inclined to deal with them if they knew about the bribery."

"Blackmail," Holmes said with a slight chuckle of his own. "Well-played, Mr. Geraghty, well-played indeed. May I ask what you intend to do now?"

"I am taking my mother and my sister, Julia, and her fiancée, William, and we are emigrating to New Zealand. My other sister, Honora, went there with her husband several years ago. She writes that it's a fine place where nobody cares where you came from, and there is much opportunity for a man to get ahead. I'll build a wharf there, as my grandfather did here."

Holmes rose to his feet and shook Michael Geraghty's hand. "I wish you all the best, sir."

I expressed similar sentiments when Geraghty shook my hand, and I stood at the window and watched him walk away down Baker Street. As I turned back from the window I said to Holmes, "You know, I am ashamed to admit that at one point I thought that that fine man could have been the murderer."

The look Holmes gave me was brooding. "You were not far wrong, my friend, I believe a Geraghty was involved in the killings."

"What?" I exclaimed. "Who?"

"Miss Julia Geraghty," Holmes replied.

I sank down into my chair. "But how? And why?"

"I do not believe she wielded the knife herself, or that she was present at all of the killings, but she was most likely present at some of them. She was certainly there at her brother's murder."

"What?" I stared at Holmes, totally aghast.

"I suspect a message was sent to John Geraghty informing him that his sister had been seen drinking at the Ten Bells. That would be enough to draw him out, with his hatred of the demon drink. He would not wish to make a scene, so he allows himself to be led from the pub by his sister into the alley, where Peter Blehane was waiting. I doubt that John Geraghty even knew that Blehane was there."

"But the other killings?"

"I suspect that Miss Geraghty was the woman that Jacky Roundhouse thought was a dollymop. She no doubt approached Harrison and drew him into the alley."

"Would Harrison have had the money for a dollymop? He was after all deeply in debt from gambling."

"I doubt she was posing as a dollymop, Watson. Tell me, my friend, if an obviously respectable young woman came up to you in the street and begged for help, what would you do?"

"I would go with her to offer what assistance I could?" I admitted.

"As would almost any man," Holmes said.

"What about Otto Bauer? Was she there for his murder? Did she lure him out into the yard?"

Holmes shook his head. "No. Otto Bauer was found in his nightclothes. He would never have gone outside in such a state of déshabillé if a woman were present."

"But why? God help me, Holmes, I do not understand why she was involved."

"The Geraghty family as a whole may not support extreme methods of gaining home rule for Ireland, but it was obvious that Miss Julia did not share her mother and her brother's opinions."

I frowned, trying to work out what Holmes meant.

"When we visited to enquire about possible Clan na Gael connections. Miss Geraghty told us about the father of the Blchanc brothers."

"He is imprisoned up north somewhere," I recalled. "Lancaster, was it?"

"Manchester. I had Lestrade enquire. The charge he was imprisoned on may well have been false, but there is no doubting his commitment to home rule," Holmes said. "Be that as it may, I found it interesting that the person most passionate about the injustice of it all was Miss Julia."

"She is a member of Clan na Gael?"

Holmes shrugged. "It is possible, but there is no evidence. Just as there is no evidence that she was involved in the murders."

I now understood just why my friend had been so dark countenanced and brooding in the immediate aftermath of the case.

"The abduction?" I asked.

"Was it truly an abduction, my friend?" Holmes asked me. "Julia Geraghty knew very well that they were not headed for Duncran Wharf. My suspicion is that that pair was running away together. I also suspect that when Michael Geraghty called out, they realized that it was all over, and Peter Blehane chose to go to the gallows alone, leaving Julia to continue the fight unsuspected."

"But you suspected," I said.

"Suspicion is all I have, Watson, and that is not enough to send a young woman to trial for her life."

"Did you mention this suspicion to anyone?"

A smile ghosted across Holmes's face. "Only Mycroft, whom I suspect is behind the greatly increased offer for Duncran Wharf."

"An offer large enough to make the long trip in relative comfort and to set up a new business in a new country?"

"Exactly. Any blackmail involved came from Mycroft, not Michael Geraghty."

"The result being that the young lady in question will be across the other side of the world and no longer Mycroft's problem," I said, marveling once again at the ingeniousness of the elder Holmes's mind.

"It is not the neat ending you prefer for your tales," Holmes observed.

I shook my head. "I will keep my notes on it only. I do not need Mycroft to tell me that publishing this story is not a good idea. Perhaps at some later date home rule for Ireland will not be an inflammatory subject. Perhaps then I will be able to publish, but until then…"

"Good old Watson," Holmes said. "What do you say to brisk stroll and a bite of lunch?"

"Sounds like a capital notion to me," I replied.

Author's Notes

The Great London Dock Strike was a real event. All the dockers and labourers downed tools and walked off the job on 14th August 1889 in protest at the pittance being offered to rapidly unload the ship the 'Lady Armstrong' at the West India Docks. Two days later the labourers on the East India Docks and the Surrey Commercial Docks joined them. By 20th August the entire Port of London had ground to a halt. Contemporary estimates suggest that as many as 100,000 men were on strike. The strike set the basis for the trade union movement which continued to make advances in workers' rights well into the twentieth century.

The famine in Ireland in the early part of the 19th century caused many families to have to make the choice between leaving or starving. Many went to London, or to Wales and Scotland. Others went further afield to Canada, the USA, Australia, or in the case of my own family, New Zealand.

Duncran Wharf did not exist. I have named it for the village, now gone, somewhere on the border of Galway and Tipperary where my family came from. As it no longer exists and I can find no trace of it on the internet, I situated it on the coast. I doubt that it was on the coast, because coastal villages tend to fare better in famine situations because of the availability of fish to eat. I sited Duncran Wharf roughly where Hermitage Steam Wharf is located.

As always I consulted quite a few books in the course of my research, the most useful being:

"Dynamite, Treason & Plot: Terrorism in Victorian and Edwardian London" by Simon Webb.

"London's Docklands: A History of the Lost Quarter" by Fiona Rule.

"Dockland Life: A Pictorial History of London's Docks 1860-2000" by Chris Ellmers and Alex Werner

"How to be a Victorian" by Ruth Goodman once again supplied me with the small details of daily life.

Sharp eyed readers will note the appearance of Inspector Edmund Reid in this novel. While he was the main character of the delightful BBC series "Ripper Street", played by the dashing Matthew Macfadyen, Edmund Reid was also a real person.

"The Man Who Hunted Jack the Ripper" by Nicholas Connell and Stewart P. Evans gave some insight into the life of this quite extraordinary man. Incidentally, Reid became a private detective after he retired. I like to think Holmes had a lot to do with that career choice.

The final book to get a lot of use was "The Victorian Dictionary of Slang and Phrase" compiled by J. Redding Ware. Unfortunately the book was originally compiled in the Edwardian era and is often extremely coy as to actual meanings to the point of being annoying. I have therefore had to double check across several language websites for the best usage. I think my usage of "dollymop" was quite clear, but if you're still confused, tallywags were testicles. Rawmaish is an Irish word meaning nonsense. "Wagtail" was another charming term for prostitute.

As usual, I have a number of people to thank.

Geri Schear for her advice on what happens when you stab someone in the kidneys. I am sure she would like me to point out that this knowledge comes from years of renal nursing.

Thanks is due to Catherine Howat for her advice on suitable German firearms of the period.

David Marcum advised me on suitable Holmesian chronologies to reference.

Finally, thanks is due once again to Steve Emecz, my publisher, and to Richard Ryan, my editor. Without these gentlemen my books would not see the light of day. Thank you.

Also from Margaret Walsh

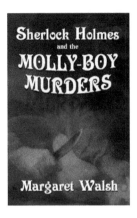

London, 1889. In a city still reeling from the depredations of Jack the Ripper another killer arises. Stalking the West End and Marylebone and striking at a seemingly unconnected group of victims, the murderer leaves fear and confusion in his wake. Mr. Sherlock Holmes, Dr. John Watson, and Inspector Lestrade face a case like no other they have yet faced. A case that will leave each of them changed and bring personal danger as they race against a mounting death toll to bring down the Molly-Boy Murderer.

Also from Margaret Walsh

When the fiancé of the sister of a Member of Parliament is found dead in mysterious circumstances, the man turns to Sherlock Holmes and John Watson to get an answer to the puzzle. Journeying to the small Wiltshire village of Barrow-upon-Kennet, Holmes and Watson are soon deep into a murder investigation. With few clues and a mounting death toll, Holmes and Watson realize that they are facing something much more sinister than a perplexed politician.

Also from MX Publishing

MX Publishing brings the best in new Sherlock Holmes novels, biographies, graphic novels and short story collections every month. With over 400 books it's the largest catalogue of new Sherlock Holmes books in the world.

We have over one hundred and fifty Holmes authors. The majority of our authors write new Holmes fiction - in all genres from very traditional pastiches through to modern novels, fantasy, crossover, children's books and humour.

In Holmes biography we have award winning historians including Alistair Duncan, Paul R Spiring, and Brian W Pugh

MX Publishing also has one of the largest communities of Holmes fans on Facebook and Twitter under @mxpublishing.

www.mxpublishing.com

Lightning Source UK Ltd.
Milton Keynes UK
UKHW011054050221
378300UK00007B/289